Skye recognized him instantly. Her heart punched against her ribs, air was vacuumed right out of her lungs and she lost the ability to move or speak. Somewhere under all that shock, she thought it strange that she did recognize Darrick McKeon. Whenever she remembered him, she pictured him in the darkness of that delicious night in the woods, and when she dreamed of him, she could never see his face.

She would feel his touch, hear his whispers, savor his attempts to protect her. She'd known him less than a full day, but the impression he'd made on her was forever.

In her secret dreams where anything was possible, she would imagine that one day he would come for her.

He turned, and for the first time she saw what he held in his arms. Babies. Two of them.

And then she saw his face, his dark glance. "How could you, Skye Fennerty? How could you not tell me?"

Dear Reader,

Okay. I'm hooked on babies. As the Jensen-Baker families swell with more and more grandchildren for Ron and me, I'm able to study and adore them while being removed from the responsibility of parenthood.

Julia is our newest addition to the family, a sturdy, bright little bundle who just had her first birthday. I've always thought she was so beautiful she should have been twins—and a writer's personal life always ends up in her books.

So I began to imagine what would have happened if Julia had been twins born to a woman who was unable at that point to provide for them. What would become of them?

Enter the pulse of every romance novel—the hero.

The twins' mother would send them to their father, but who was he? My imagination created three possibilities, and when I couldn't decide among them, the McKeon brothers were born.

I leave you to decide WHO'S THE DADDY? Darrick, the hospital administrator, Dillon, the orthopedist, or Duncan, the actor?

Muriel

Muriel Jensen

Daddy By Default

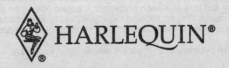

HARLEQUIN®

TORONTO • NEW YORK • LONDON
AMSTERDAM • PARIS • SYDNEY • HAMBURG
STOCKHOLM • ATHENS • TOKYO • MILAN • MADRID
PRAGUE • WARSAW • BUDAPEST • AUCKLAND

To Julie Marie Baker—a true Angel Baby

ISBN 0-373-16737-7

DADDY BY DEFAULT

Chapter One

Darrick McKeon strode rapidly through the Emergency entrance to Valley Memorial Hospital. If he could have made himself invisible, he would have. He was anxious to get in and out without being stopped by a crisis in Supply, a staff grievance or a request by the reigning orthopedist for yet another piece of equipment with a multimillion dollar price tag.

There was always more activity in the ER than elsewhere in the hospital, so everyone was too busy to notice him.

Yes! He'd made it past the gift shop and the cafeteria. One more long corridor to the administrative offices and he could get his golf clubs and be out of here for three weeks.

He didn't intend to check his messages or look through his mail. He'd already given up three precious days of his vacation to attend the Northwest Hospital Association conference on security held in Seattle.

He'd found it a more effective method of sedation than sodium thiopental. Valley Memorial already had the finest and most consistent security of any hospital its size, but the board had considered it important for morale and image that Valley Memorial's administrator attend. And a large part of his life was dedicated to keeping the board happy.

His office was half a corridor away. He was going to make it.

Darrick picked up his pace, grateful that Bev wouldn't be there on a Sunday afternoon to slow his progress. His secretary was hardworking and devoted, even heroic, but since her husband had left her a year ago with four children under ten, she was like Pauly Shore on steroids. And he didn't want her following him around the office, trying to apprise him of every new development in the hospital—among the patients and the staff—when all he wanted was to retrieve his golf clubs. He was dedicated to his job, but after a year of arbitrating departmental rivalries over budget money, he needed his vacation.

"Darrick!"

"Mr. McKeon!"

"*Mr.* McKeon!"

Rats! Caught. And from three sides.

Darrick stopped at the end of the corridor. His office door had been flung open and Bev stood in the doorway, looking shocked and condemning.

Ellen Brock, head nurse in Obstetrics, approached him from one side. She was built like a defensive lineman, and Darrick got the distinct impression she was waiting for any sign that he was going to try to rush past her.

Will Champion, OBGYN, approached him from the other side. There was confusion and sympathy in his face.

It took Darrick a moment to realize that this was not just an alliance formed to ruin his free time. They all looked upset and angry about something.

"What is it?" he asked, looking from face to face. He stopped at Bev's. "What are you doing here on a Sunday?"

"Trying to find you," she replied a little stiffly.

That didn't make sense. "But you knew where I was. You had the phone number of the conference center. You knew I was due back this afternoon."

Brock came to stand in front of him. "Why didn't you answer your cell phone?"

"Because," he replied patiently, "I'm officially on vacation. My parents are a thousand miles away, my brothers and sister are distributed around the globe and usually beyond the reach of the telephone, and thanks to this hospital, I have no time for a social life. Therefore—any call would be business and I'm—all together now—on vacation!"

He pushed past Bev into his office. "So, I don't know what the problem is, but I'm really not here. If you're having a crisis, you should be lying in wait for Paul Miller. The director of finance is in charge while I'm gone."

He went straight to the closet for his clubs, slung the bag over his shoulder and turned to find his doorway blocked by three determined bodies.

"I thought you were different," Brock said judiciously.

Bev closed the office door. "How could you, Mr. McKeon?" she asked in a faltering voice.

Will sighed. "You're going to have to do something about it now, buddy. Particularly since she's gone."

Darrick dropped the bag to the floor and propped it against his desk, accepting that he wasn't going to get out of here without finding out what this was all about and getting Miller in here himself.

"Different from what?" he asked, perching on a corner of his desk. "How could I what? And do something about *what?*" Then, remembering Will's last remark, he frowned. "Gone as in...dead? Who?"

Ellen Brock came forward to look him in the eye. "Different from other *men*. You come on as though you have respect and concern for the women you work with, then you go and..."

Bev pushed her aside and confronted him. "I was always proud to work for you, and when you made the tough decisions, I backed you up. But true integrity goes beyond the job and into the bedroom!"

While he wondered what in the hell that meant, Will stepped between him and Bev. "Not gone as in dead," he clarified. "Gone as in ran away."

"Who," Darrick demanded, "is gone?"

Will jammed his hands in his pockets and shrugged a shoulder. "She was admitted as Rachel Whitney, but we can't find any evidence to back up her identity. She said she didn't have insurance, but gave us a large cash deposit. And now she's gone."

"And the deposit didn't cover the procedure?"

"Yes. It covered it." He frowned at Darrick as though watching his face for evidence of something. "But she left them here when she took off."

Darrick still couldn't grasp the problem. "Left what?"

"The twins."

This was going to come together for him any minute; he was sure of it. He just had to ask the right question. "Okay." Darrick ignored the women and concentrated on Will. "You're telling me that a woman was admitted under an assumed name, gave birth to twins and subsequently abandoned them?"

Will still wore that watchful look. "Yes. That's exactly what I'm saying."

"Well, that's an Adult and Family Services problem." Darrick was beginning to see a light at the end of the tunnel. Except that Will had seen this sort of thing happen before. Why was it creating such a trauma this time? "You know the procedure. Make sure the babies are healthy, call AFS, and they'll try to find out who the father is."

"We know who the father is." Bev took a few steps closer. "Rachel Whitney Whoever did put the father's name on the birth certificates."

He frowned at her. "Well, call him."

Brock wedged her way in between Will and Bev. "We did. But he didn't answer his *cell phone.*"

Darrick prided himself on being quick-witted. He had an MBA from Stanford, had brought Valley Memorial out of the red during the six years of his administration and had personally made a small fortune on the stock market when everyone else was losing money.

So why didn't he understand what Brock was telling him?

Will put a hand on his shoulder, apparently taking pity on him. "She listed D. K. McKeon as the father, Darrick. That's you."

All right. That was clear enough. He remained still while the words registered. And remaining still wasn't easy when one's blood pressure rose fifty points and one's heart went into ventricular fibrillation.

He had a baby? Twins? No. Oh, no.

"Would you like oxygen?" Brock asked, an edge of sarcasm to her voice. "Or shall I just get a crash cart?"

"Wait a minute." Darrick struggled to think clearly. "Is D. K. McKeon all that's on the birth certificate?"

Will took a step back as Darrick got to his feet. "What do you mean?"

"I mean, there isn't a full first name? Does it say Darrick K. McKeon?"

"No, but you're..."

"Yes, I'm D. K. McKeon," Darrick interrupted. "But I have two brothers, Dillon and Duncan, both with the middle initial *K*."

Brock blinked, then considered a moment. "But you're the one who is administrator of this hospital where the mystery woman left her babies. She probably just put your initials because she knew everyone would know who you were."

Okay. Oxygen was getting to his brain now. He was beginning to put things together. "Were the babies full term?" he asked.

"Thirty-four weeks," Brock replied crisply. "But they were perfect."

Thirty-four weeks. That put conception of the babies at about the second or third week in September. Maddie Hale had left in July to take the teaching job in Virginia, and he hadn't had a relationship since.

Dillon, however, ran a clinic, but traveled from one global crisis to another with the Northwest Medical Team, and he had a George Clooney reputation. He was fearless and reckless.

Duncan, on the other hand, went from one movie set to another, and everyone knew that actors often became so engrossed in their roles that even they couldn't tell reality from fantasy. And if Darrick's memory served, early last fall Duncan had been in Mexico filming with Yvette Delacourt. He'd portrayed a suave but lethal villain in love with a border guard's wife.

The beautiful movie star *might* have abandoned a baby rather than put her career on hiatus while she stayed home with it.

But how likely was that? Studios no longer tried to protect pristine images—there weren't any. And if she had given birth, why would she have done it in Portland rather than Los Angeles?

If Dillon had impregnated a nurse or doctor on his team, would she have come to this particular hospital to have the babies, intending to abandon them to his brother?

He didn't know what to think. Nothing made sense. Everything he suggested to himself was likely, but it was easy to come up with counterarguments.

"What did the mother look like?" Darrick asked. Yvette Delacourt had been in the last Batman movie. Certainly someone would have recognized her. "Tall, slender blonde with killer blue eyes?"

Will raised both eyebrows at that description. "No. Brunette with long hair. Average height and build. Very quiet."

Darrick shook his head. Didn't sound like any woman he'd had anything to do—

His private claim to innocence was banished instantly by the image of a beautiful brunette whose body had appeared average. But making love to her had turned out to be anything but.

He hadn't remembered her because he'd been thinking in terms of relationships. And Skye Fennerty had been a one-night stand. Actually, a one-night flight. Or, more correctly, a crash.

This couldn't be, he thought, knowing even as his

mind formed the words that it could. Lives, fortunes, destinies often changed dramatically on the turn of a forbidden moment.

And he'd had one last September 14. He remembered the date specifically because he'd been on his way to his parents' fortieth wedding anniversary in Skye's twin-engine, modified bomber. But fate had had other plans.

He ran a hand down his face to try to conceal the complicated emotion ricocheting inside him—confusion, anger, wonder, possession, and then anger again.

"Where are the babies?" he demanded of Will.

"We have them in Pedes," Will replied, exchanging an uncertain glance with his companions.

Bev and Brock were studying him, apparently confused by his confusion.

He walked purposefully past them, headed for the nursery. He passed the viewing window before he reached the double doors and stopped to look. In the front row on the right side were two babies so tiny they occupied the same isolette. And like some wonder of nature in babies generally considered too young to relate to their surroundings—their inch-long little hands were linked. The twins. He noticed that with a blow to his heart. He took it as a sign that they knew they'd been abandoned and had decided that survival required that they join forces.

He understood that feeling. It spoke to him. The McKeon siblings had always been that way, and even when they'd lost six-year-old Donovan, his spirit remained woven into each one of them, alive and significant in their hearts.

And these babies had shared a womb. What was it like, he wondered, to share the elemental darkness of prebirth—to know life together even before life knows you?

"Come on." Will caught his arm and drew him toward the doors. "I'll introduce you to your daughters. Your…their mother named them."

Brock and Bev followed them inside.

A pretty young nurse with brown hair caught back in a bun, gently untangled the tiny fingers and placed one of the babies in Darrick's arms.

"Ah…" He tried to resist, prepared to explain that holding babies had never been part of his job description, but Brock had bent Darrick's arm to receive the baby.

"This is Michelle," the young nurse said, smoothing the pink blanket in which the baby was wrapped. She indicated the hospital bracelet. "They're so identical, we have to read who's who."

Darrick noticed the baby's warmth against him and the clean fragrance of talcum. But he felt no weight in his arms. The other baby looked no bigger.

That was confirmed for him the next moment when Will took the first baby from him and the young nurse put the second one in his arm.

"And this is Gabrielle," she said. "We've been calling them the angel babies because they're named after two of the archangels. Aren't they beautiful?"

They were. Though every little detail of feature and limb was in miniature, the babies were exquisite. Feathery dark hair stood up in little Mohawks above blotchy but plump cheeks, button noses, Cupid's bow mouths. Perfect little fingers moved gracefully in sleep.

"Are they…big enough?" Darrick asked Will.

"Five pounds each, give or take an ounce," Will

replied with a smile. "Very good for twins. And the rash is only temporary. It'll be gone in a few days."

"You taking them home with you?" Brock asked aggressively.

Darrick felt the clutch of panic in his chest. He could live without three weeks at Salishan Lodge, golfing, but what was he going to do with two infants?

There was no woman in residence at his place, and his mother was a thousand miles away. He'd seen women defeated by one baby. What was he going to do with two?

And he had no crib, no…no…whatever else it took to keep babies happy.

"I have a bassinet you can borrow," Bev said helpfully, suddenly more smiling than judgmental. "And an infant seat." Then she frowned suddenly. "Though you'll need two of those."

"I can get you a second one so you can get the babies home," Brock said briskly. "The auxiliary's donated a few just for that purpose."

Darrick knew he was experiencing shock, but he heard himself tell his secretary and the busybody nurse that he would appreciate their help. Then he watched Will and the young nurse put the babies back in the isolette, and like the split screen on a state-of-the-art television, he saw his life crumble and dissolve on the other screen.

Babies. Two of them. His. God.

Now that the babies were together again, their hands moved unerringly toward each other's and they linked fingers in their sleep.

In the space of an hour and a half Brock fitted his car with two infant seats while Bev went home to get the bassinet and promised to meet him at his place.

The Pediatrics Department donated blankets and diapers, bottles and formula and a few other necessities. Will put the babies, who were still sound asleep, in the infant seats, and he and Bev and Brock and most of the Pedes Department and first-floor staff stood around to wave him off as though he were leaving for an Olympics competition—or some fatal secret mission.

In the fifteen minutes it took him to get home to a quiet country house on a shady little lane on the edge of town, one baby awoke and quickly woke the other.

They screamed in unison, urgent, desperate cries that made him certain he'd lose them to asphyxiation before he even got them home.

Bev ran out of his house to meet him, took one of the babies, infant seat and all, and hurried inside with it. He did the same with the other and found her in the kitchen, the infant seat propped on the island countertop while she gave the baby a bottle.

As he placed his twin beside the one she fed, Bev held out another bottle. He took it, put the nipple at the baby's lips, and the deafening screaming stopped. He couldn't believe it. The silence seemed to ring around him.

He leaned wearily on an elbow as he held the bottle. He'd had the twins for an hour and a half, everyone else had done everything for him, and he was already exhausted.

"What are you going to do?" Bev asked him with concern. "How are you going to deal with two infants by yourself?"

He had no idea.

"I don't suppose you saw the babies' mother?" he asked.

She shook her head. "I didn't know anything about this until this afternoon, when Brock called me in because the woman had run off and they'd spotted your name on the birth certificates. They thought I might be able to reach you." She hesitated a moment then asked quietly, "So, they are yours?"

He knew he had to say it out loud to believe it—to find a way to deal with it. "They could be," he admitted. "But if they are, their mother never said a word to me."

"Men," Bev said with a judicious shake of her head. "You fool around and never look back."

The ironic thing, Darrick thought, not bothering to counter her accusation aloud, was that he'd never behaved like that. He'd never been into keeping sexual accounts and setting records, and he'd never been irresponsible or deliberately careless.

Except the night of September 14. And then, when he'd finally reached his parents' house, he'd called Skye several times and left messages, but she'd never returned his calls. He'd tried again when he'd gotten home, but her continued silence forced him to conclude that that night hadn't meant as much to her as it had to him. So he'd put her out of his mind.

He stared at the baby sucking greedily on the bottle and tried to imagine Skye Fennerty simply walking away from her and her twin. He couldn't.

But then, he'd only known Skye all of about twenty-four hours.

Bev glanced at the clock.

"I'm sorry this ruined your Sunday with your kids," Darrick said guiltily. "I'll see that you get a full day's overtime."

"It's all right," she said wryly. "I'll go home as

soon as we get them back to sleep. You're the one who's in for a nightmare couple of weeks.''

"Mmm. Good thing I'm on vacation, or I'd have probably had to bring them to the office for you to file or something.'' That was gallows humor, he knew. Otherwise, he didn't feel as though he had an amused bone in his body.

Bev showed him how to burp the babies, then rock them back to sleep. She gave him a book she claimed contained every fact he would need to know about the care of infants and left him her phone number at home and told him he could call her at any time.

Then she left.

Darrick stood in the middle of his empty, silent house and experienced the impact of knowing his life had been changed forever. It was like a one-two punch that had driven him to his knees.

He'd felt this overwhelmed only once before in his life, and that had been when he was seven. His little brother Donovan had died, and no amount of screaming and pleading on anyone's part—even his father's—had had the power to bring him back.

"All right," he told himself bracingly. "You've got a few more years on you since then and considerably more experience. You know you have an intellect and a determination you can trust. They always come through for you. You can do this.''

Right. He could do this. First thing on the agenda was to call his mother and see if she would fly down to help him until he could do the second thing on his agenda. That was to find Skye Fennerty and find out what in the hell she thought she was doing.

HIS MOTHER'S VOICE was breathless. "Did you come running up from the basement?'' Darrick asked conversationally.

"No, I just ran in from the car because I forgot the tickets, of all things!" She laughed. It always righted the world somewhat to hear her laugh. "Good timing, Darrick! One minute later and your father and I would have been on our way to Las Vegas. What is it, love?"

Another trip. His parents were enjoying their retirement by taking off on small trips whenever the spirit moved them. And it did often.

He couldn't spoil it for them, and he couldn't squeeze the news that they might be grandparents into a two-minute conversation. "Nothing, Mom." He forced a light tone of voice. "I was just checking on you. Wondering if you've heard anything from Dillon or Duncan."

"No, we haven't. Far as we know, Dillon and his staff are still out of touch somewhere in Nicaragua, and according to the schedule Duncan left us, he's somewhere on a tributary of the Nile and won't be finished filming for another couple of weeks. Why? Did you need them for something?"

"No," he denied quickly. "Just trying to keep up with everybody." He heard a horn honk in the background. "You'd better go. Say hi to Dad."

"Darrick…?"

"Love you, Mom. Put a couple of bucks in the dollar machine for me, would you?"

"Of course." She hesitated a moment. "You're sure there was nothing particular you wanted to talk about? Dori should be back from London in a couple of days."

"Great," he said, praying that was true. "Maybe she'll stop by. Call me when you come back. Bye."

Darrick went to pour himself a cup of coffee. Then he wandered back into the living room and made himself deal with the reality that, for a while at least, he was going to have to cope with the crisis of fatherhood alone.

Neither of his brothers would be back for a couple of weeks, and even if the twins did belong to one of them, he was the designated caretaker until they came home.

Well, he thought drily, listening to the silence, he might make it if the babies slept for three weeks.

He took the cordless phone off the desk, settled into a comfortable chair and asked the information operator for the number of the Mariposa Airport, Fennerty Air Service's base of operations.

"Fennerty's out of town for a few days," the small airport's manager told him when he dialed the number. "She's due back day after tomorrow. Can I give her a message?"

"Thanks," Darrick said. "I'll just call back."

He turned off the phone and laid it on the arm of his chair. That had been surprisingly easy. He'd had visions of having to trace Skye Fennerty across the country to find her. But she was still in Mariposa.

The day after tomorrow he was going to make her wish she wasn't.

Chapter Two

Darrick had met Skye Fennerty when the doctor friend who'd been flying him to San Diego for his parent's fortieth anniversary party was radioed that a sudden change in a patient's condition required that he return to the hospital.

He had landed at Klamath Falls, Oregon, just long enough to drop Darrick off, on the chance he could pick up a commuter flight there.

Darrick was explaining his situation to a clerk behind the counter when he felt a tap on his shoulder. He turned to find a young woman standing behind him in khaki coveralls and baseball cap.

"I'll take you to San Diego," she said. She had wide blue eyes, a dewy complexion, and smiling lips the color of Merlot.

For a moment he was speechless, wondering if she was just a stranded male traveler's fantasy.

"For a hundred dollars," she said with a grin, "and a guarantee that you don't get airsick."

He gave her the cash and the promise right then and there.

"All right," she said briskly, extending her hand. "Skye Fennerty, Fennerty Air Service."

He'd shaken her hand and introduced himself, liking her solid grip. "Skye?" he asked. "You made up that name when you became a pilot, didn't you?"

"No." She took his bag and led the way across the terminal. "I come from a family of pilots whose name rather conveniently was Schuyler. No male heirs last generation, so when I came along, I was called Schuyler to keep the name alive. It looks good on freight-hauling contracts to have a pilot named Skye."

"I come from a tenacious family like that," he'd said, following her out of the terminal and across the tarmac to a lineup of small planes.

"Really?" She'd stopped at what appeared to be an old bomber and turned to face him, her expression innocent. "Your family was alcoholic and dysfunctional, too?"

"Ah...no. Unless loving Vegas and bad antiques can be considered dysfunctional."

She'd laughed, opened the passenger door and pulled down the air stairs. "Nah. I love Las Vegas, and nothing from the past with a story attached to it can be bad. Climb aboard, Mr. McKeon. We're off to San Diego."

He'd followed her into the plane. "Ah...we're not going to bomb anyone on the way, are we?"

She shook her head. "That's extra." Then she laughed. "My little tracker bomber was a real steal, and I modified it for hauling freight. No leather-lined interior, but you'll be comfortable."

And everything had gone beautifully until a strange little knocking sound caused her to stiffen visibly while she consulted meters and gauges.

"What?" he asked.

She was frowning and manipulating knobs and

switches. "Something that never happens," she said. "Fuel pump failure, I think. Looks like you're just not meant to make that party, Mr. McKeon."

He'd struggled against an impulse to wrestle the controls from her, reminding himself that he didn't know anything about airplanes and that it was no time to indulge the distinctively male compulsion to take over.

He sat quietly in his seat, praying that his parents' anniversary celebration wouldn't be marred by the news that their second child, who'd tried so hard to get there, was now permanently part of the Central California landscape.

"I'm afraid we're going to make an unscheduled stop," she said finally, with a smiling glance at him.

If she could smile, so could he. His macho was at stake. "Are we going to survive it?"

"I survive everything," she replied, and he knew instinctively she wasn't talking about other crashes. She flung a hand out that landed on his stomach.

He realized in an instant that she was checking his seat belt, but his body reacted as though she'd had other plans entirely.

Then they were going down, down, down, and for his own sanity's sake he watched Skye rather than the approaching earth. The plane leveled out, and they were skimming the sandy landscape at a speed that seemed far too rapid for landing.

He remembered thinking philosophically that that was life. Many times and in many ways you were forced to land long before you were ready. Like Donovan.

As they touched down and bounced up again, still going much too fast as they approached a thick stand of trees, Darrick wondered if he was going to see Donovan again after all this time.

Then the trees were upon them, there was a roar and a vicious impact, and everything went black.

He'd awakened, hanging upside down like a drying bunch of weeds, the top of his head brushing the cockpit ceiling. He'd struggled to remember what had led him to this predicament when a high-pitched little moan close beside him brought it all back. Skye Fennerty had landed them safely as she'd promised. Upside down in a tree, but safe.

He'd stretched a hand out to her and she'd grasped it. "Tommy," she'd said, holding tightly to him. "Tommy, are you back?"

In her upside-down position, her hair streamed toward the roof of the plane and her eyes looked vague. Her hands went to her seat belt, trying to find the buckle.

"No, don't," he'd said, unbuckling his own belt and pushing his door open. "We're in a tree. Hold on a minute."

He'd reached out of the plane, caught a fistful of branch and turned himself right side up. They'd lost a wing and were jammed pretty snugly among trunks and branches. It was fifteen or twenty feet down a very sturdy pine. A glance in the direction from which they'd hit showed that they'd lopped off the tops of a quarter mile of forest.

He leaned back into the plane where Skye was fiddling with the radio, still hanging upside down in her seat.

"Dead," she reported. Then she smiled thinly. "Did you say that I've landed you up a tree?"

He'd been relieved to hear the wry humor in her

voice. "Yes, but don't worry. Being up a tree is a familiar situation for me. Now I see why you wanted your one hundred bucks up front."

"I have a pack with a cell phone in it." She pointed behind her. "In a leather satchel. See it?"

He groped behind her on the ceiling-turned-floor and found it. He hooked it on a branch of the tree, then reached for her. "Let's get out of this tree and try to figure out where we are. I'm not real optimistic we'll be able to pick up a signal to call for help, though."

Her eyes were dark with urgency as he held her tightly and helped her get her balance on the thick branch. "I filed a flight plan. They'll look for us. But I am sorry about your parents' party."

Her dismay over the party, considering the somewhat desperate nature of their circumstances, surprised him. Then he remembered what she'd said about her family.

"It's all right," he'd assured her. "I'm sure the fact that you managed to save my life will balance out their annoyance that I didn't show up."

They'd had to climb just a few yards down the tree to the bottom branch, then there had been a seven- or eight-foot drop to a bed of pine needles.

Darrick had leaped to the ground first, reached up to catch the pack Skye tossed, then opened his arms for her.

It had surprised him when she'd clung to the branch and looked uncertain. She'd just landed a malfunctioning plane on a mountaintop without batting an eye. Now he couldn't get her to jump out of a tree.

"Skye, you're only eight feet up," he'd reminded

her. "That's not much worse than standing on top of your plane."

"I never stand on my plane."

"Your porch railing, then."

"I live in an apartment." Then she frowned at him. "Who stands on their porch railing?"

"Kids do. Didn't you?"

"No. But I hid in the tree outside my bedroom window when my father was drunk." She blew her bangs out of her face, trying, he guessed, to look nonchalant. It didn't work. She looked just as she might have as a frightened child. "It seemed like a very long way down then. And it still does."

"Okay, look." He decided a change of perspective was needed here. "Don't think about the taking off, think about the landing. I'm here to catch you. Think of me as O'Hare International Airport."

"O'Hare has more accidents per…"

"All right!" He'd stopped her abruptly before she could finish the thought. "Where do you keep your plane?"

"The Mariposa Airport."

"Then I'm the Mariposa Airport. Come on." He spread both arms and waggled his fingers invitingly. "All runways open."

"I hate thi-i-i-is!" she'd moaned. But she'd jumped and he'd caught her squarely and held his stance so that she landed in his arms and clung for one long, undisturbed moment.

He understood instinctively that something within her needed that moment, and that it had to do with more than jumping out of the tree and landing safely. Perhaps it was an expression of the fear she'd felt, but had been unable to show, when she'd had to land the plane.

He wasn't sure what it meant. He knew only that she needed him and that he liked that.

Unable to find a signal to use the cell phone, they spent the night in the woods under the shelter of a tarp she kept in her pack.

They split a thermos filled with an aromatic mocha she'd bought from a coffee vendor at the airport in Klamath Falls.

They were huddled together using the tarp as a blanket, and she'd smiled up at him in the darkness. "I'm sorry you missed your parents' party," she'd said softly, "but I'm glad I'm not out here alone."

He'd squeezed her closer, the immediacy and intimacy of their situation eliminating the caution that usually marked a first encounter.

"Me, too," he'd teased. "I'd hate to wake up upside down in a plane and discover that there was no one else to blame for it."

She'd backhanded him in the chest, he'd caught her hand and kissed it, then her eyes had met his in the darkness.

He remembered an overwhelming need to feel her lips against his. And when he did, they were just as he'd imagined—cool, supple, sweet, eager.

Then need had fed upon need, and before he could put logical thought in gear....

A STEADY, nerve-rending sound dragged Darrick out of his dreams. He opened his eyes, surprised to find himself in his own living room rather than in the shadowy dusk of a mountaintop woods.

He realized that cries had awakened him. Baby

cries. Short, staccato bursts of the most demanding sound. He raced toward it, wondering desperately what he would do when he got there.

By 4:00 a.m. Darrick began to see a pattern to the angel babies' activities. They slept for two hours, then woke up screaming. They ate greedily, made alarming noises while he held and burped them, screamed while he changed them, then fell asleep again.

The only problem was that they didn't sleep for the same two hours. If he was lucky, the sleeping periods overlapped for a few minutes. Otherwise Michelle was screaming while he fed and changed Gabrielle, or the other way around.

By 6:00 a.m., when both babies were screaming, he prayed that they did belong to one of his brothers and that he would survive this to present them to whoever came home first.

Now desperate for sleep himself, he wished for a rocking chair in which he could sit with both babies and hopefully get them and himself to sleep for the same two hours.

Then he remembered the front porch swing. He endured several more moments of screeching while he bundled up both babies against the early-morning chill, wrapped himself in a blanket and went onto the porch. He didn't have a hand free to close the front door, but he didn't care.

He sat in the middle of the swing, propped his feet on the porch railing and began the back-and-forth rhythm. In a matter of minutes both babies were asleep.

With a groan he let his head fall back against the cushions and closed his eyes.

He awoke to the sure knowledge that he was being

watched. But before he bothered to open his eyes, he told himself that there was no one around but the babies, and, according to Bev, they couldn't see anything farther away than a foot, and the distance from their faces to his was more than that.

Besides, if they were awake he felt sure they'd make that fact known to him.

He tried to doze off again while listening to the subtle sounds of his country neighborhood coming awake. He heard an alarm clock next door, the slap of a newspaper against a stair, the bark of a dog announcing to one and all that he was officially on duty.

But the feeling of being watched persisted. He opened one eye and saw a small dark-haired young woman in jeans and an Oxford sweatshirt sitting on the railing near his feet, smiling at him.

He'd have wept with relief, but he was too exhausted.

"Dorianne," he said wearily, lifting his head. "My favorite little sister. How are you, baby?"

"I'm your *only* little sister, and I'm fine," she said, leaping gracefully to her feet and coming to lean over the twins. "But what in the hell are you doing with two babies?"

He frowned at her. "I thought Dill and I cured you of swearing ten years ago?"

She glanced up from her admiration of the angelic little faces to give him a devilish one. "Don't try to change the subject, Darrick. Where did you get these babies?"

"The hospital," he replied, closing his eyes again. "I came home from a weekend conference on security to find that they'd been left with my name on them."

"What do you mean, your name on them?"

"D. K. McKeon was the father's name on the birth certificate."

"But..."

"I know. Dillon and Duncan are both clever enough to be out of the country and out of reach." He sighed and raised his head again. "But...there is a chance they're mine."

"How?" she asked, then, reconsidering, changed her question to, "I guess I mean *who?*"

Michelle stirred restlessly.

"Oh-oh," Darrick said. "Take cover. Michelle's waking up."

Dorianne took the squirming baby from him, held her to her shoulder and began to pace the length of the porch. "How do you tell which baby is which?" she asked. "They're so identical."

"The nurses in the hospital colored Michelle's thumbnail with a skin scribe. It's a nontoxic marker used to illustrate the skin for surgery or treatments."

"Good thinking. You were about to tell me who the babies' mother might be." She gave him a questioning look as she passed him. "I didn't know you were seeing anyone."

Darrick let his right arm fall slack, finally free of the five-pound weight that after an almost sleepless night felt like five hundred. Gabrielle slept on peacefully.

"I'm not," he said, carefully shifting position. He winced as his abused muscles protested. "But...there was the pilot who was flying me to Mom and Dad's anniversary party when we went down in the Siskiyous."

"You're—" She began at full voice, then remembering the baby at her shoulder, turned it to a whisper as she stopped in front of him. "You're kidding! You'd crashed in a plane, climbed down a tree, taken shelter under a tarp and were still in the mood to...?"

He watched her as she struggled for a word. "Make the best of it?" he asked. "Yes. We were. You've spent too long in an academic environment, Dori. The outside world is filled with passion."

Her lips tightened and he knew he'd hit a nerve. He hadn't meant to, but he studied her, fascinated to discover something new about the little sister who was still somewhat of a mystery to the rest of her family.

"Please don't preach to me, Darrick," she said, resuming the scrappy-kid-sister persona with which she seemed more comfortable.

"I wasn't preaching," he said mildly. "Just observing. Do you want to know about her or not?"

With Michelle now quiet in her arms, Dori sat beside him. They rocked together in the early-morning quiet.

"What's her name? You didn't tell us much about her that weekend, you just kept calling her."

"Skye Fennerty."

Dori made a face. "You're kidding me? A pilot named Skye?"

"I know. That's what I said." He told her the story about the Schuyler name.

"What's she look like?"

"A lot like you," he said with a grinning glance. "Only prettier and taller."

She sighed. "Who isn't? But a nice older brother concerned with my self-esteem would never point that out."

"That would be Duncan," Darrick said. "Unfortunately, you're talking to me."

"Yes, but we're talking about *her*," Dori said, "so could we please get back on track? What's she like?"

He remembered clearly what he'd thought of Skye Fennerty on that mountaintop. "Brave, witty, charming, vulnerable."

Dori turned slightly to face him, her eyes troubled. "Good qualities, but nothing really…substantial."

He had to admit that with a nod. "True. But I only knew her for twenty-two hours."

"Yet, you made twins with her."

"Maybe."

"And you haven't seen her since?"

He shrugged his free shoulder helplessly. "I called and left messages, but she never called back. I just figured she didn't want anything more to do with me."

"Well…pardon me, but she seems to have *gotten* more. But where is she? I mean, if these are her babies, why isn't she here? If she's that brave, would she have taken off and abandoned her children?"

Darrick had thought about that during the few quiet moments he'd had during the night, but he hadn't been able to concentrate sufficiently to explain or excuse that behavior.

"I wouldn't have thought so, yet—" he indicated the twins "—here I am. I called the airport she flies out of and she's due back tomorrow. I'm going down to see her."

"But what about the babies?"

"I'm taking them with me. If they are hers, they make a stronger case."

"For what?"

"For her to be a mother to her daughters. Maybe she just needs to know I'll provide financial support."

Dori studied him, frowned, then shook her head. "I can't believe this. What if they're not hers?"

"Then they're not mine, either." Gabrielle began to fuss, and Darrick lifted her to his shoulder as Dori had done with Michelle. "They're Dillon's or Duncan's. But since they're both out of reach, I'm it until one of them comes home. Incidentally what are you doing here? Mom told me you were coming home, but I thought she meant home to San Diego."

"Daddy faxed me that they were going to Vegas," she replied, "so I thought I'd come and see you for a few days and relax before I start working on my thesis on novelists of the nineteenth century."

"Dori," Darrick said on a sudden inspiration. "You're like a gift from heaven!"

She studied him doubtfully. "Isn't that contrary to everything you've ever told me?"

He swiped the air with his free hand in a gesture of erasure. "That's in the past. How would you like to spend the summer here playing nanny for me until we find out without a doubt who Michelle and Gabrielle belong to? I'll pay you more than nanny scale, and you can work on your paper when the girls are sleeping. And if I ever recover my health after last night, I might even give you one day off a week."

She considered. "One day off," she said finally. "I could report you to the Department of Labor."

He looked heavenward in supplication. "And I could tell Mom about Benny Candalaria, but I haven't yet, have I?"

She sighed, but her shoulders stiffened. "No, you haven't, and you won't if you want to live to be a father to these babies."

"Then let's work together here," he suggested calmly.

He could see her brain at work in her wide, dark eyes. "My computer's in San Diego," she said, "And it's out of date."

He got the message. "I'll buy you a new one," he promised. "A laptop, too, if you like."

She gave him a greedy smile and offered her hand to shake on the deal. "You may call me Nanny Fine."

Gabrielle, unhappy with Darrick's attempts to soothe her, began to cry in earnest. Michelle, apparently in sympathy, joined in.

Darrick walked and bounced the babies in the living room while Dori warmed formula and prepared bottles. She fed one baby while he fed the other, then helped him put them to sleep in the bassinet.

It was the first time he'd been without a baby in his arms since midnight.

He swept his sister into a bear hug. "Bless you, Dori!" he said emphatically. "I thank the impulse that brought you here instead of home to Mom and Dad."

She hugged him back. "You're welcome." Then she pushed him away to arm's length and told him firmly, "I want a Hitachi MX Notebook with all kinds of goodies on it."

He nodded amenably. "You can have two—today, even—if I can have four hours sleep before you go shopping."

"Deal."

MARIPOSA WAS on the northern California coast, a small, grassy field between Highway 101 and the Trinity National Forest.

"Mariposa means butterfly," Dori read from a bro-

chure as Darrick drove the Toyota he'd rented at Eureka, the babies asleep in their infant seats in the back.
"Apparently a couple of guys who didn't do well in
the gold fields came here and started a hotel."

"If they didn't do well in the gold fields," Darrick
asked practically, "what did they build a hotel with?"

"The dream to do it, I imagine," she replied, swat-
ting him with the brochure. "You know, it's entirely
possible that Air Fennerty…"

"*Skye* Fennerty," Darrick corrected, taking the brochure from her and dropping it in the built-in pocket
on his door. "Fennerty Air Service."

"That Skye Fennerty," Dori continued, "didn't return your calls because you always respond practically, even in an impractical situation."

He took offense to the suggestion. "Money happens
to be a very practical element in the construction of a
hotel."

"But the dream is more essential. You can borrow
the money, but you can't borrow the dream."

Darrick glanced at her over his shoulder. "You're
nuts. How far would the twins get on a dream when
the ultimate outcome of their lives depends upon food
and shelter, a good education and the right opportu-
nities?"

Dori pointed to the sign that indicated the entrance
to the airport. He turned.

"If that was all they needed," she asked, "why are
we here trying to find their mother? If she is their
mother. If they are your babies."

"Because she'd be better able to raise them than I
am."

The narrow, paved road led to a string of well-kept
but simple, no-frills hangars. A square building beside

it with one large window appeared to be a terminal. A tattered windsock hung limply above it.

Fennerty Air Service was clearly stenciled in sky blue paint on the only hangar in the lineup that was white rather than battleship gray. Visible through the open bay was a plane that looked about the same vintage as the Grumman.

"It doesn't look to me like she has money for all those things," Dori observed as Darrick pulled up in front of the white hangar.

"I have the money," Darrick said, turning off the motor. "So she can afford to have the dream. Will you give me a hand here, please?"

SKYE FENNERTY studied the unsigned contract before her on the counter in the terminal's coffee shop. *Financial security,* she thought, ignoring the pen that sat beside the contract. *At last.*

The merchants' associations of Mariposa, Belvedere and San Cristo had formed a purchasing alliance and hired her to freight their goods from Los Angeles and San Francisco, citing the excellence of her past performance in serving several individual businesses in the group.

She waited for the thrill of satisfaction to fill her and make her life worthwhile. But it didn't.

She knew why, of course. Satisfaction in life was not supposed to be derived from business success—at least, not entirely.

It should come from supportive parents, a loving husband, children. But she'd been forced to give up on all those things. Her parents had been like textbook cases of the results of alcohol abuse, her ex-husband,

Tommy Fennerty, had walked out of her life, and she'd had to turn her back on motherhood.

Business was all she had left.

But life went on, and she had to find another way to make it worthwhile. She picked up the pen.

"Skye!"

She turned to the terminal's double doors as a short, round man in a rumpled white shirt and tie and shiny dark pants called her name.

"Someone to see you," he said around the stub of cigar in his mouth. "He's waiting in your hangar."

Marty Clements, the Mariposa Airport manager, held one of the doors open while Skye folded the contract and tucked it into the breast pocket of her jumpsuit. She did half a revolution on the stool and leaped off.

She was several inches taller than Marty and patted his head affectionately as she went through the door.

"Thanks," she said. "One of my new clients?"

He shook his head and hurried along beside her as she headed for the hangar. "Nobody I recognize," he said, then pulled her to a stop to ask worriedly, "You aren't going to move your plane to Eureka after you sign that contract, are you? I can't afford to lose you, Skye. And on top of that, I don't *want* to lose you. You sure you don't want to marry me?"

Skye laughed and hooked an arm around Marty's shoulders and pulled him along with her as she walked on. His proposals were a running joke between them.

"I'm not going anywhere, Marty. You mean Margaret's finally going to give you that divorce?"

He looked relieved. "No," he removed the cigar from his mouth and waggled his eyebrows. "But I could get her to agree to let you live with us as wife number two.''

''Thanks, when I get to be a wife again,'' she said, pushing him gently toward his office door as they passed it, ''I'd have to be number one. See you later.''

Skye saw the back of the man walking around her plane and recognized him instantly. Her heart punched against her ribs, air was vacuumed right out of her lungs, and the ability to move or speak fled entirely.

Somewhere under the shock of seeing Darrick McKeon, for the first time in all those months, Skye thought it strange that she recognized him. Whenever she remembered him, she pictured him in the darkness of that delicious night in the woods, and when she dreamed of him, she could never see his face.

She would feel his touch, hear his whispers, savor his thoughtful attempts to protect her and make her comfortable, when few people in her experience had ever done that for her.

She'd known him less than a full day, but the impression he'd made on her was forever.

In her secret dreams, where anything was possible, she'd imagined that one day he would come for her. A little shiver ran through her at the possibility that that was why he was here.

He turned, apparently suddenly aware of her, and she saw for the first time what he held in his arms. Babies! Two of them!

The sight reactivated her body's functions and brought a smile to her lips as she went toward him.

''Darrick...?'' she began, putting a hand to each cherubic, sleeping little face.

Darrick interrupted her with an emphatic and drawn-out, ''Oh-h-h God.'' His head fell back for an instant, he closed his eyes and said it again. "God. Oh, God."

It didn't seem to be a curse, but rather a sort of plea.

Then he seemed to recover, expelling a sigh and looking from one baby to the other, then to her with a darkly condemning glance.

"What do you have to say for yourself, Skye Fennerty?" he demanded quietly.

She stared at him.

"How could you not tell me you were pregnant with *my* babies," he went on, "come to my hospital to have them, then abandon them without a backward look? How have you lived with yourself the past three days?"

Skye looked around herself to make sure she wasn't hallucinating. No. She had both feet on the ground. She was surrounded by many things she recognized. Darrick McKeon was standing here, just inches away from her, just as she'd imagined him for months. She couldn't speak.

"Thanks to you," he said, "everyone at the hospital thinks I left you alone to cope any way you could, and that you left me the babies out of desperation."

She shook her head, opening her mouth to reply, but he was still talking.

"What in God's name made you think I wouldn't care?" he asked, a note of injury in his voice making her look from the babies to him. "I called you repeatedly. I left a dozen messages which you chose to ignore after leading me to believe that—" He stopped abruptly and drew a breath that seemed to allow him to turn his thoughts in another direction. "All right. That doesn't matter now. What matters are the twins.

I'm prepared to see that all three of you are comfortable. That night you told me you live in an apartment.''

"Yes."

"We'll move you out of there and into a house. We'll talk about what you need and decide on a monthly sum. Of course, that would be adjustable for special needs...."

He stopped, probably noticing that Skye was distracted by the red thumbnail on a tiny hand rubbing a little nose.

His voice quieted, became less severe and more conversational. "The nurses in OB did that so we could tell Michelle from Gabrielle. Here.'' He held his arm toward her so that she could take Michelle.

Skye took the baby from him and held her to her shoulder, supporting the tiny head with her other hand as the baby seemed to be studying her face with my-opic interest.

Skye wanted to hold the babies more than she wanted anything else in life at that moment.

"Hi, sweetheart,'' she crooned, absorbing the freshly powdered smell of the baby, the warm, light weight in her arms. The twin yawned mightily and Skye laughed.

She looked from the baby's face to Darrick's. "She already has a square chin like yours,'' she said, relishing the wonder of new life. "And lots of dark hair."

"The dark hair could come from you,'' he said, then offered her Gabrielle while he reclaimed Michelle.

"Darrick," she began again, but Gabrielle began to scream, and Skye stopped and turned her attention to quieting her.

"Can I do anything, Darrick?'' A pretty young

woman in jeans and a simple red sweater walked into the hangar.

Skye felt an instant and virulent stab of jealousy as the dreamy quality of this encounter began to disintegrate. So. He was bringing the babies to her because he had someone else.

"Skye," Darrick said, drawing the young woman toward him with his free arm. "I'd like you to meet my sister, Dorianne. She's hired on as nanny. Dori, Skye Fennerty."

Skye smiled at her, inordinately pleased to learn that Dori was his sister. But judging by the suspicious look Dori returned, Darrick's sister wasn't at all pleased to meet her.

Skye understood her reluctance and nodded politely anyway. "I'm pleased to meet you."

Dori came and scooped the baby from her, that look still in place. "Why don't I take her so you and Darrick can talk? We'll sit in the car." She smiled thinly at her brother. "I'll be right back for Michelle."

Darrick excused himself and followed his sister with the second twin. Skye watched while he leaned into the back to put the baby in the infant seat. He spoke briefly to Dori then loped back to the hangar.

"Is there somewhere we can talk?" he asked Skye.

"Ah…we…"

"Just hear me out," he said, interrupting her again. "Let me tell you what I want to do about you and the twins."

She found it impossible to resist that offer. "All right," she said. "We'll sit in the back booth in the terminal coffee shop."

Chapter Three

And that was how everything she'd thought she'd lost was restored. She'd intended merely to listen, to fantasize about how her future *could* change, and then she was going to follow her original plan to become an airfreight mogul.

But Darrick told her that when he'd first learned about the twins, he'd tried to blame one of his brothers, who also bore the D. K. initials. "I can't reach them, because one's with a Red Cross team in Central America, and the other's filming in Africa. They're not due back for a couple of weeks, so I couldn't check out who the babies belong to from that angle. But…there was you. And you were the only woman I'd been with eight months ago." He sat opposite her in the booth and traced the rim of his cup with a long index finger. Then he drew his hand back, folded his arms on the table and looked her in the eye. "They're yours."

His gaze mesmerized her. It was filled with kindness and compassion and a wonderful intensity that had made her feel so alive that night on the mountain. It had the same effect on her now.

"I'll take care of you," he said. "Just tell me what

you think you'll need, and I'll provide it.'' He leaned back in the booth, his legs sprawled out under the table so that she had to tuck hers under her. ''I'll be involved as little or as much as you're comfortable with.'' He studied her with a faint smile then said with an amused self-deprecation that touched her, ''I presume since you didn't return my calls, that means you weren't very impressed with me, so I imagine you'd prefer that I make myself scarce.''

She couldn't let him believe that, because now she was certain. She wanted the babies. And she wanted him.

''I felt quite the contrary,'' she said, meeting his surprised gaze evenly. ''I *was* impressed, but I thought it was…safer…to let it be just one of those things.''

''Why safer?'' he asked.

That was easy enough to explain. ''I told you a little about it that night. Because my parents drank and fought until my mother died and my father disappeared when I was eighteen—and I spent most of my time staying out of the way—I know how families should behave, but I've never experienced it myself. And I had a feeling that with you…'' She was afraid this might be too much honesty, but she said it anyway. ''That our relationship would become something important and…eventually, being part of a family might become an issue. I have no unresolved anger or anything. I came to the conclusion as a girl that it saps energy and holds you in one place. But I guess I have a problem with unresolved…love. I think that probably makes me poor family material.''

That darkness in the back of his eyes seemed to clear and he asked in surprise, ''Is that why you left the twins with me? Skye, I saw you in action and you're very brave and clear thinking and very…giving.''

She felt her color deepen at the memory of just how giving she'd been on that mountain. She saw him take notice of that and squared her shoulders as she began to formulate a framework for the future she'd given up on—until he'd walked into her hangar only moments ago.

''You said you'd be willing to be involved as little or as much as I wanted,'' she said.

He measured her with a look, apparently realizing that their conversation was taking a sudden turn. ''That's right.''

''What do you mean by 'as much'?'' she asked intrepidly.

He didn't move a muscle, but she saw something subtle change in his eyes. He was more watchful suddenly, more alert. ''What did you have in mind?'' he asked.

She did her best to appear bold rather than terrified. ''I think marriage would be best for the babies,'' she said in a rush. ''For stability and security and…all that.''

She finished lamely, alarmed by the fact that he did not react. He looked neither horrified by the suggestion, nor thrilled with it.

''Married,'' he repeated.

''Yes,'' she said.

Darrick made himself think, because he couldn't begin to analyze what he felt. For a man who felt strongly but never let feelings determine action, this was a dangerous moment.

All he could assess with any accuracy was how beautiful she was. He'd remembered her and dreamed her, but it had been the feel of her in his arms that lived with him, the generosity and the trust with which she'd made love with him. And he'd remembered a curious shadow in the back of her eyes behind the courage and the laughter and the whispers of his name. Had that been her past?

He'd been surprised when she hadn't returned his calls, and finally began to believe that he'd imagined the intimacy of their connection.

But now she was telling him that it had been there all along—that he'd been right. And only her unwillingness to burden him with a less-than-perfect woman had prevented her from calling him back.

He wondered if that was true, or if she just wanted a home for herself and the twins.

But he'd made it clear he'd be willing to care financially for all three of them. She could have had security without having to deal with him.

Maybe she hadn't understood that. "You can have whatever you want," he said, resting his forearms on the table and leaning toward her, "without my involvement."

Her expression remained fixed but that dark area in her eyes seemed to move forward. "So, you'd prefer not to be involved?" she asked.

"I just want you to understand," he corrected, "that I don't have to be."

She leaned toward him, blue eyes intense. "But you said you would be involved as little or as *much* as I wanted. And I want as much as I can get for my babies. That would include you. I don't want them feeling that there's a door closed between them and their father like I always felt. I want them to be embraced, cherished, loved."

He held her gaze. "Then all you want is a father for the twins."

She didn't blink. "No. I'd like a husband if you're still the same warm, old-fashioned kind of man you were the night we spent together."

He was momentarily diverted. "Old-fashioned?" he asked, thinking that was a quality he'd never expected to hear defining him.

She smiled at his change of expression. "It's a compliment."

"In what way?"

Her smile warmed him and he felt it inside like a sip of brandy. "In a way that I still remember," she said quietly. "It was clear that your experience was the big city, probably a big cushy office somewhere, yet after the crash, you took charge to find shelter, to build a fire, to make me feel protected and safe until we could get help."

He pardoned his behavior with a grin. "I'm a victim of parents who are young at heart but whose souls live in the nineteenth century."

She nodded. "You told me that night. Your father taught history at Crest College, and your mother taught nineteenth century literature."

"So the age of women wanting to be considered equally capable and equally competent is over?"

She considered him with a look that was so tender and so…indulgent that for a moment he felt boneless.

"Not at all," she said. "But you didn't make me feel inferior, you made me feel special. That's a skill in taking charge most men don't possess."

He was rapidly beginning to see things her way. "What would you do about your plane?"

She looked startled. That was a detail she apparently

hadn't considered. "I guess," she said with a wry smile, "that it'd be more practical for me to go with you to Portland, than for you to stay here with me and become a freight jockey."

He nodded seriously. "Considering I can't pilot a plane, I think you're right."

She looked wistfully around the terminal's coffee shop, and he wondered if she was thinking about how much she would miss the little airport. Then she focused on him. "So—are you the same man?"

"I can't promise," he admitted frankly. "If you're doing what you're supposed to do with life, every experience changes you a little, and it *has* been almost a year." He grinned. "But if it's any comfort, I do still like to take charge. If you still find that a charming quality, we should get along fine."

She laughed lightly. "As long as you understand that while I might find it charming, I probably won't feel called upon to let you do it every time."

"Fair enough." He pulled a bill out of his wallet to pay for the coffee. "I've never been married before, or had babies, so it might take me a while to get the hang of it."

She slid out of her side of the booth as he got to his feet. "You have forty-eight hours more experience with being a parent than I do. But I was married once."

They faced each other as they stood beside the table. "To Tommy?" he asked.

She went instantly pale. "How do you know about Tommy?"

"After the crash," he said, trying to analyze that reaction, "you called me Tommy when I touched you to see if you were all right. You asked me if I was back.''

"Oh." She put both hands in the pockets of her jumpsuit and studied the floor, as though she needed a moment to recover. "Another pilot," she said finally, raising her eyes to him and shrugging a shoulder. "Didn't last very long. He left me."

"I'm sorry."

She shrugged again. "Marriage is a gamble. You never really know what you've got—or *who* you've got—until it's too late."

He frowned. "You're sure you want to do it again?"

She heaved a deep sigh and smiled at him. It amazed him that she could keep pulling up that sunny smile again and again. With the dysfunctional family she'd claimed and the husband who'd left her, she should be ill-tempered and cross.

"I keep thinking I've given up on finding happiness," she said ingenuously, "then something happens that makes me want to give it another try. Are you sure *you* want to take the chance?"

He didn't have to think about it. She had remembered him, after all. Of course, he'd given her twins; it wasn't likely she'd have forgotten him. But he believed her when she told him why she hadn't returned his calls. There was something important between them besides the babies, and they had to explore it.

"I'm sure," he replied.

She led the way out into the sunshine.

"I'll take my sister and the babies back to the motel," he said, walking her to her hangar. "If you can square things up with your plane and your business this afternoon, I'll come back to pick you up tonight and we'll pack your things. Maybe arrange to store whatever you don't want to bring along. We can fly home as soon as you can get your business settled."

She looked a little stunned.

"Do you need more time?" he asked.

She blinked, and he could see plans forming in her eyes. "I was just about to sign a freight contract," she said, "but I think I can work that out with some friends who'd be glad to take it over." She smiled. "And I could fly us home. I have to get my plane there, anyway. Or I could meet you there if you have round-trip tickets."

"I wasn't sure how long it would take us to talk it out," he said, "so I haven't booked a return flight." He grinned. "Could you check the fuel pump before we leave?"

She gave him a reproachful look. "I always check everything. That was a fluke or…fate."

"Big-time." He saw that look of concern fill her eyes again. "You look worried."

"Well…yes," she admitted candidly. "Aren't you? I mean, less than an hour ago I was alone."

"You must have known," he suggested mildly, "when you left the twins and put my name on the birth certificate, that I'd come looking for you."

"Yes." She stopped in front of the open doors of her hangar. "I guess I just didn't expect such an attractive offer."

"I want it established now," he said, "that *you* proposed to *me*. So that if it all falls apart, it's your fault. Or if it works and we're celebrating our thirtieth anniversary and someone asks how we got together, I can tell them that you crashed me in a plane, stranded me on a mountaintop, seduced me, then proposed marriage. Because the fact that it all happened in the first place *was* your fault.''

She folded her arms, amusement replacing her concerns. ''I seduced you?'' she asked skeptically. ''That's not how I remember it.''

''You suffered a blow to the head,'' he reminded. ''You can't be expected to remember the details.''

''Oh, I remember them,'' she insisted. ''You held me in your arms, you recited poetry to me, you…''

''You brought the plane down like Amelia Earhart herself.'' He interrupted her with a teasingly judicious look. ''But you were afraid to jump out of the tree. And you didn't like the coyote noises very much, either. You kept holding on to me. That's why I recited poetry to you. You were tough but you still needed me. I found that more seductive than black lingerie and spiked heels.''

Skye had no idea what to say to that. Though she teased him about it, all she could remember was how mutual it had all been—how safe and right it had felt when they'd begun, and how changed she'd felt when it was over.

Making love with Darrick McKeon had restored hope in her. But when he'd called her the following day from his parents' place, all she'd been able to think about was that her family had seen to it that there was no love in her past, and Tommy had made her believe there could be no love in her future.

''What is your family going to think about this?'' she asked worriedly. ''You made them sound so wonderful that night, what are they going to think about the twins being left at the hospital and me…proposing marriage?''

He put a hand to her upper arm. She felt the warm

imprint of every fingertip but did her best not to betray how important it made the moment for her.

"I told you my brothers are away," he said, "and my parents are gone for a few days. They don't know the twins were left at the hospital, and I don't think they have to." He grinned. "And the 'who proposed to whom' is just for my personal satisfaction. We'll tell them I proposed to you. But they'd be pretty upset if we had a wedding without them."

He made the handling of touchy details sound easy. She indicated the car behind him in which his sister sat with the twins. "I don't think Dori approves of me."

"We're all very protective of each other." He glanced toward the car with a smile. Dori held her wrist up to the window and tapped on the face of her watch. He turned back to Skye. "Butting into another sibling's or a parent's business is a family trait. We're not happy unless we're interfering. I'll make her understand. And speaking of Dori, she's working on a dissertation for her master's degree. So, when I wasn't sure if I'd be able to find you, or even if the twins *were* ours, and I was afraid I'd have to deal with them all alone, I asked her to stay with me as the twins' nanny in exchange for room and board and an outrageous salary. I hate to—"

"I'd like her to stay," Skye put in quickly. Much as she wanted the twins, she hadn't had very much to do with babies and was terrified of the prospect of being alone with them. "If you think she'd *want* to. I'll need help until I understand what they need."

He seemed first surprised then pleased. "Good. I'll talk to her about it. I'll be back at six."

"I'll be waiting."

Skye watched Darrick drive away, knowing it was too late to ask herself if what she was doing was wise. But she did anyway. She'd proposed marriage to the man with whom she'd spent an unforgettable night eight months ago. That was insane.

"No, it isn't," she told herself firmly. It was a sign of the wellspring of hope that lived in her and had led her on a search for love that so far had simply taken her from one dark vacuum to another.

But now it had given her babies. And Darrick McKeon. How could she not embrace them?

She would be a good wife and mother. And he must have thought so, or he wouldn't have come looking for her.

It occurred to her that he might have just wanted to get the babies off his hands. But he could have put them up for adoption and not gone to the trouble of finding her if that were the case.

No. She had a good feeling about this. The four of them would be fine together. Five of them, including Dori.

Common sense tried to tell her she was kidding herself.

But common sense had little to do with love and happiness, she thought, as she listened to the familiar sounds of her lonely little life:

A small Zenith trainer revved as it started down the runway. Jim and Joey Barber, in the hangar next door, fought over splitting the proceeds of their small air service, and Marty called out to Whitey Snow, who ran the coffee shop and had stepped outside for a smoke, to save him a blue-plate special for dinner.

That was pretty much the extent of her circle of friends. They were loyal and true, but at night they all had someone else to go home to. She didn't, and she was tired of it.

She folded her arms and looked skyward into the clouds, where she was so comfortable and where she'd found a small measure of happiness when earth and her parents became too much to bear.

"Okay, I imagine You could sometimes take issue with the way I do things," she said quietly, "but You said to love one another, only You've sent me so little to work with. So I'm presuming You're having second thoughts about that and You've prepared this opportunity to make it right, so I'm taking it. Please accept my thanks in advance, just in case it doesn't work out."

Then she went to ask the Barber Brothers if they'd like to run freight for the merchants' association.

"I THINK YOU'RE INSANE," Dori said. It was 2:00 a.m. and she was walking and bouncing a screaming twin while Darrick walked and bounced the other. They'd opened the door that connected their motel rooms to make dealing with the babies easier.

"That's called transference," Darrick whispered loudly. His baby had miraculously fallen asleep, and he didn't want to shout in her ear. "You're nuts, so you think everyone around you is nuts."

"You spent one night and one day with her and now you're getting married?"

"Dori, we made two babies together."

"Yes, but you don't *know* each other. What if she turns out to be a witch?"

"She isn't."

"You can't know that on twenty-four hours' acquaintance."

"I can. And I do."

"You're acting out of desperation." The baby in her arms quieted a little between screams, and Dori stopped walking and began rocking instead.

"I'm doing what I want to do," he said quietly but insistently. "So butt out, okay?"

"Well, I don't like it."

"You don't have to." He went to the portable crib in the corner of his room and put Gabrielle down in it and waited for her to awaken suddenly and scream a protest. She didn't. He went back to Dori. "On second thought," he said. "You do."

She studied him suspiciously as she continued to rock. The baby's screams had turned to soft whimpers and were now quieting altogether. "Why?" she asked.

"Because she wants you to stay on."

Dori glowered at him, then carried Michelle to the crib and put her down beside her twin. She, too, remained asleep.

Darrick caught Dori's arm, drew her back into her room and said with quiet emphasis, "She doesn't know any more about babies than I do, and she says she'd be grateful for your help. This way you'll have more free time for your dissertation."

"How do you know," Dori asked stubbornly, "that she isn't after you just for your bucks?"

He drew a breath for patience. "Because I offered her money for her and the twins. It would have been easier for her to take it and not have to deal with me."

That seemed to force her into a reevaluation. She sank wearily onto the edge of her simple double bed. "Mom and Dad are going to freak."

They might, but he preferred to think positively.

"They'll be thrilled to have a wedding in the family at last. Not to mention grandchildren."

"I just hope you know what you're doing." There was a worried note in her voice.

"I always know what I'm doing," he assured her.

"That's in business, Darrick. This is relationships. Maddie took a job across the country because you couldn't give her enough time in your life, remember?"

He shrugged philosophically. "She wanted a playmate, not a serious relationship."

"Most women want a serious relationship with a man who can also be a playmate." She tossed her blankets back and climbed into them. "Remember that I told you that."

He pulled the blankets up to her chin as he'd done so many times when she was little and he'd baby-sat while his parents taught night classes. "Shut up and go to sleep."

"You've been telling me that for twenty years," she complained sleepily.

He flipped her light off. "Isn't it time you listened?" He pulled her door partially closed as he went back into his room where the twins remained fast asleep, hand in hand.

Chapter Four

Darrick's home looked comfortable, Skye thought, even from the car. It sat alone on one side of a tree-lined block of old turn-of-the-century homes a mile outside of Edenfield, just west of Portland, Oregon. She'd left her plane at Foxglove Field, halfway between Portland and the small suburb. It was late afternoon, and the street had a fairy-tale, sun-dappled quality.

The two-story white house was hip roofed, giving it a barnlike appearance. Red shutters were open on many small-paned windows, and a white picket fence enclosed a stone walkway that led to a covered portico. A single-story wing protruded from the middle of the side of the structure. The far end of it was clearly the garage.

"Watch your step on the walk," Darrick advised. He held a carrier in each hand and followed Skye and Dori to the door under the portico. "Dori, you want to use your key? I have my hands full."

Dori, who'd been polite but virtually silent all the way from the airport, shifted her laptop carrier to her other hand and dug into a small purse over her shoul-

der. She turned a key in the lock and stepped back
with a sweep of her hand to let Skye in first.

A high-ceilinged foyer papered in white linen
greeted her with a gold-framed mirrored reflection of
her face. She'd caught her hair up in a knot in an
attempt to feel more mature and maternal.

But her reflection looked wide-eyed, pink-cheeked
and terrified, so she looked away and followed rich
green carpeting into a large living area.

It was clearly decorated to masculine tastes, yet remained warm and welcoming. Open-beamed ceilings
and windows through which sunlight poured gave the
creamy color of the walls a warm glow.

A long sofa was upholstered in a green, red and
cream plaid and stood under a collection of faded old
signs and polished harness fittings. On the opposite
wall was a wide stone fireplace with a collection of
tankards on the oak slab mantel.

A wing chair in green-and-white check flanked one
side of the fireplace, and on the other was a fussy old
settee in dark wood, upholstered in balding tapestry.

Skye's gaze stopped on it. Fussy finials came to two
sort of Gothic points and struck a discordant note in
a room that seemed otherwise comfortably perfect.

"A gift from my parents," Darrick explained rue-
fully as he placed both carriers on the sofa. The babies
slept peacefully. "They love to go antiquing, but
they've filled their home with some of the most in-
credibly ugly stuff you'll ever find anywhere, so now
they're starting on their children. Well, me, really, because I'm the only one who's always home."

She traced the turn of the wood with her fingertips.
"How wonderful that they think of you when they're
out shopping."

"Wonderful?" he asked doubtfully.

"Yes." She leaned over the settee to touch the worn fabric. "If they thought it was beautiful, it makes it beautiful. When it's reupholstered in a light fabric, it'll fit in better and look...great."

Dori winced at her as she put her laptop down on a chair. "Oh, no. You're a Pollyanna, aren't you?"

Darrick rolled his eyes at his sister's assessment. "She's in graduate school," he said to Skye. "It isn't cool to be hopeful."

"I'm hopeful," Dori said, "that people will deal with reality. We can't solve the world's problems otherwise."

Skye nodded. "You're right. But you have to start with your own problems, and the way they keep reappearing you have to be hopeful. Otherwise you'd give up."

Dori raised a haughty eyebrow and fixed a disapproving look on Skye. She was making her suspicions known in small, subtle ways, and while Skye didn't entirely blame her, she knew she had to begin to deal with it soon to make her place in Darrick's household.

Dori turned to Darrick. "I'll take the babies upstairs," she said.

"No, I'll do it," Skye countered quietly. "Then I'll make some coffee and see if I can find something to fix for dinner."

"Daredevil pilot *and* Suzy Homemaker, too?" Dori asked.

"Neither," Skye replied. "I flew freight up and down the West Coast. That's hardly daredevil stuff. And I'm just a so-so cook."

Dori took a step closer to Skye. This was clearly a confrontation. "But Darrick told me how fearless you were in landing the plane on a little strip of mountaintop. Or were you just showing off for him?''

Skye answered without raising her voice. ''Well, you know, it was that pesky hopeful thing again. I didn't want to die. If you consider saving Darrick's life showing off for him, I guess I did.''

''And making love with him on a few hours' acquaintance and after a plane crash wasn't a daredevil stunt?''

''Okay, that's it.'' Darrick caught Dori's arm and would have hauled her out of the room, but Skye stopped him.

''That was a fair question,'' she said when he turned to her in surprise.

''It was an outrageous question!'' he replied angrily. ''And none of her—''

''It *is* her business,'' Skye insisted. ''She's just concerned about you. And it isn't fair to brush her off because she's your little sister.''

''Don't think you're going to get to me,'' Dori snapped at Skye, ''by defending me to him!''

Skye took Dori's arm and smiled at Darrick. ''Where's the kitchen?''

He pointed back the way they'd come in. ''Just follow the hall in the other direction.'' Then he grinned. ''Don't cook her. I don't understand it, but my parents are fond of her.''

''I'm convinced that one day I will be, too,'' Skye replied with a dry expression, ''but not today. We'll be right back.''

The kitchen was a large square room, also with open beams. The cupboards were white, the walls, pale blue and the countertops and kitchen island were covered with blue-and-white tiles.

Skye took in the warmth of it while gently but firmly pushing her soon-to-be sister-in-law into one of four white captain's chairs pulled up to the work island.

She took the chair beside her. "All right, rip into me," she challenged. "Tell me what's on your mind."

Dori seemed willing to take advantage of the opportunity. "What's on my mind," she said, "is that there's something on yours. What's your game, Skye?"

"Game?" Skye asked.

"You're not the twins' mother, are you?" Dori pierced her with dark, probing eyes. "You just saw a way to make a buck and marry well and you took it."

"No," Skye denied quietly. "I saw a way to unite the four of us and took it."

Dori studied her grimly. "If you love him, you'd have returned his calls in the beginning."

"My reasons for that are personal," Skye replied. "I might explain myself to a friend, but not to someone determined to be hostile."

"I'm 'determined' to see that my brother doesn't get hurt. He's organized and systematic and something of a genius in business, but under that is a trusting soul." Dori leaned toward her threateningly. "If you cause him one bad moment, this whole family will come down on you so hard you won't know what happened until you're ninety!"

Skye believed her. "My intention," she said, "is to make him happy. I love him and the babies, so you'll just have to make room for me in the family circle."

"We'll see about that when my parents get here."

A fussy cry sounded from the living room.

Skye granted with a nod the possibility that Darrick's parents would be upset. Then she stood. "Meanwhile, the twins are hungry." Dori's eyes went to Skye's unimpressive chest with a tauntingly questioning look. "Not very bosomy for a woman who had twins five days ago."

Skye forced herself to remain polite. "I was given a medication because I knew I wouldn't be breast-feeding."

"Because you knew you'd be abandoning your babies?"

"No, because I decided, when I knew I was carrying twins, that breastfeeding would be too difficult."

Dori stared at her a long moment then apparently decided that was believable.

"You're not what I wanted for Darrick," Dori said with a sincere disappointment Skye found painful.

To pay her back for that, Skye replied, "Well, I'd have preferred a trusting, sweet-natured aunt for my daughters, but I guess we have to take what we can get."

Dori sat up, clearly affronted. "What I think of you would never affect how I treat them."

"I know that. But they'll sense the tension and that's harmful."

"All right!" Dori huffed in frustrated anger and got to her feet. "I'll be civil to you," she said, wearing a very uncivilized expression, "but you'd better watch your step."

"I'm a pilot," Skye replied easily. "I never make a move that isn't carefully calculated, then double-checked. Relax, Dori. Let's try to enjoy your summer here."

Dori spread her arms helplessly, growled and stormed away.

Skye went wearily back to the living room to find Darrick feeding one of the twins. He had one knee squared on the other and Michelle—no, Gabrielle—cuddled in his left arm.

He looked up from his task, a questioning smile in place. "You two establish a hierarchy?" he asked.

Skye noted the expert way he held the bottle up to the light to see how much milk had been consumed. He'd learned a lot in a very short time. That somehow lightened the grim feeling left from her conversation with Dori.

"I think it's futile for the time being," she said. "She'll just have to get used to me."

Darrick nodded, then pointed the bottle at the infant seat beside him where Michelle was just beginning to fuss. "Grab a bottle. She's waking up, too."

Skye reached into a small cooler at his feet where they'd put the twins' bottles for the drive home. She was about to head back to the kitchen to warm it, but he pointed her to the step-back cupboard in a far corner of the room.

"Open the double doors on top," he said. "There's a microwave. Just a couple of seconds seems to do it."

"My goodness," she said over her shoulder as she followed his instructions. "Such convenience."

"You wouldn't want to take the chance of missing a winning run on TV by having to go into the kitchen to microwave the popcorn."

"You'd have to go for the cola, anyway."

"Nope." He pointed with the bottle to the bottom of the cupboard. "Other half's storage and a small refrigerator."

Gabrielle squealed at him, demanding her bottle

back. He laughed as Skye sat beside him with Michelle in her arms. "Gabby will appreciate having food at her fingertips. She seems to eat nonstop."

"Did Dori go out?" Skye asked, offering Michelle the bottle. The perfect little bow mouth opened and took in the nipple.

"She's bringing our bags in," he said. There was the sound of a loud thud in the foyer. Darrick grinned at Skye. "That was probably yours. No crystal in it, I hope?"

"No crystal."

There was another thud.

"That was yours," Skye said, "because you're collaborating with the enemy." A third thud sounded through the house. "But, what was that?"

"Hers, just because she's mad." He laughed lightly. "Always was a fierce little kid. Very sweet when things go her way, and an absolute devil when they don't."

"In all fairness, that could describe me. Or you."

"It's hard for me to imagine you slamming things around." He sent her a teasing glance. "Except a plane, of course. You've developed a new method for topping trees the logging industry might be interested in. And when you're finished, the toothpicks are already made. No need for a factory."

She made a face at him. "What do you want for dinner?"

He drew the bottle from Gabrielle's mouth and put her to his shoulder. "That sounded very domestic." He frowned. "You don't think this is it, do you? The daredevil pilot and the hospital administrator become the Cleavers?"

She shook her head. "I don't think so. Besides, they

had two boys. We have two girls. Why?'' He turned to face her, still patting the baby, and she turned toward him, Michelle in her arms still eating greedily. ''Are you afraid of becoming a middle-American suburbanite?''

Sun poured through the window, warming their faces and putting glossy highlights in his dark hair. It lit the depths of his eyes, too, and she looked for fear there. But all she found was amusement.

''No, I don't think so,'' he replied. ''In its way, it sounds rather attractive. I've always been the careful one. Maybe it's a middle child thing—keep your eye on the older one so he won't get too far ahead of you. And on the younger one, so he won't get hurt trying to follow.''

''But there are four of you,'' she pointed out. ''There really isn't a middle child.''

Something shifted in his eyes, and where there had been amusement there was now a trace of sadness. ''Actually, there were five. We had a brother Donovan who died at six of leukemia.''

She felt the sadness herself. She'd never had a sibling, but she could well imagine the grief of losing one.

''I'm sorry. You never said…''

''His name comes up most often when we're all together. He was gone before Dori was even born. So for a few years, there were just three of us, Duncan and Dillon and me.''

Gabrielle belched loudly, putting an end to the suddenly serious turn in the discussion.

''Isn't it interesting,'' he said, ''that we wait for the burp in babies, but we're horrified when eight-year-old boys do it?''

"That sounds," she speculated, helping him change the subject, "like you remember horrifying people in just that way when you were eight."

"Very astute of you." He placed Gabrielle on a blanket across his lap and rubbed her back. "We were all pretty good, but Dillon was the best."

"The actor?"

"The doctor. He maintained that the technique was to down two twelve-ounce colas in five minutes. And they had to be canned. The stuff on tap's too diluted."

She nodded gravely. "So this became a scientific study?"

"Dillon already had a medical turn of mind."

"And what were your findings?"

"That three boys, hiding in the tulip tree and belching in concert at the family's Fourth of July barbecue, could be made to apologize individually to everyone assembled and then grounded for a week."

"Those autocratic parents again."

"Right." He smiled thoughtfully and Skye found herself jealous of his memories. There'd been pain there certainly when Donovan had died, but they'd had each other to lean on and to learn to laugh with again.

After every crisis in her life, she'd had to teach herself to laugh all over again.

The quiet moment was interrupted by the sound of something heavy bumping on every step as Dori apparently carried up one bag after another.

"Dori changed the order of things when she arrived," Darrick said. "Before she came, our whole lives were about being in competition with each other. Then, suddenly, we were allied to protect and guide this scrawny little firebrand who probably didn't need our interference at all, but we'd made a pact the day we first saw her in the hospital and we carried it through.''

Skye smiled at him. She'd longed her whole life for someone who would want to protect and guide her. ''No wonder she loves you so much.''

With a suddenness that stole the breath from her, he touched her hair. A tendril had broken free of her pins, and he tucked it behind her ear. Then he ran a thumb along the hairline at her temple.

''She has to understand that my protection now extends to you and the babies, as well, so she has to be careful how she treats you.''

Then he lowered his hand and the moment was over. But it had held a loving touch and a promise of...protection. That wasn't as good as love, but it was more than she'd ever had before.

She decided then and there that whatever risks were involved in this relationship, they'd already been paid for.

When Michelle finished her bottle, Darrick took Skye and the babies upstairs. They peered into two guest rooms, one in green, one in blue, and a bathroom with a ball and claw tub and an old shower ring above it that held pearlescent curtains that matched the flower on dark blue wallpaper.

Darrick indicated a closed door behind which the voice of Rod Stewart could be heard singing about a heart beating like a drum.

''Dori's room when she visits,'' he said, then led her into the master bedroom at the end of the hall. It held a four-poster double bed with an antique-looking trunk at the foot of it. There was a tall dresser, a wardrobe closet with louvered doors, and a Boston rocker near a window.

Across the room was a bassinet and a changing table.

"Friends at the hospital provided us with the baby furniture," Darrick said.

Provided *us*… Skye liked the way that sounded. She went to touch the white wicker bassinet that looked like new. "A close family and good friends. You're so lucky."

She went to the window and found that it looked out onto the sunset over the tree-lined street and the lush green lawn.

"What a view," Skye said quietly, holding Michelle up to look out. "Look at that, Michelle. Isn't that pretty?"

Darrick came up behind her with Gabrielle in his arms. "Yeah, it's pretty," he said, as though he hadn't really thought about it before. "But it's just the street."

She shook her head, unable to stop staring at it. "It's rooftops and chimneys, the tops of trees and the bellies of clouds." She sighed. "My window has always looked out on an airport."

She came out of her thoughts when she became aware of the silence. He was staring at her, a smile twisting a corner of his lips. "The *bellies* of clouds?" he asked.

"Sure," she said, forcing a straight face. "When you fly, you have a different relationship with the clouds because you…you interact with them. They have faces and limbs and…bellies."

"I see." He shook his head with what appeared to be wonder, his eyes perusing her face with great interest. "You are as amazing as I remember," he said.

She could barely breathe. "So are you," she whispered.

Darrick leaned over the babies, put a hand to the back of her head and kissed her. It was a gentle kiss, a gesture of reacquaintance. That night of the crash, the danger they'd faced and their relative safety under the circumstances had heightened their perceptions and their emotions, and when Darrick had built a fire and taken her in his arms, their kisses had been instantly explosive.

But this was a different communication. The babies were a reminder that that passion existed, but this kiss was a beginning to all the discoveries there hadn't been time for then.

And it was a revelation to Skye that touch could say so much. She'd never been physically abused but she'd always been neglected, and she'd felt most of her childhood and a lot of her adult life as though her skin lived in anticipation of a touch offered in kindness or concern or simple affection.

But it had come so seldom. Occasionally from a teacher, or someone at the airport who had felt sorry for the skinny waif who haunted the terminal.

She swore she felt his fingerprints on her as his hand slid gently down the side of her neck to her shoulder.

The breast near his hand tingled with expectation.

Then he sighed and raised his head. His dark eyes were rueful. "Lovemaking is out of the question for a couple of months, isn't it?" he asked.

"Yes," she replied, color filling her cheeks. It was only part embarrassment. The other part was disappointment. "Six weeks."

He groaned softly and led the way downstairs.

They placed the now-sleeping babies in the portable

crib at one end of the kitchen and worked together making salads and sandwiches.

Dori joined them for dinner and an amicable conversation about the wedding.

"We'll get blood tests tomorrow," Darrick said. "Then we'll get married at the courthouse. Is that all right?"

"Ah…blood tests at the hospital?" she asked.

"No," he replied. "At my brother's clinic."

"But Dillon and Duncan aren't here to stand up for you," Dori said.

"I'll ask Dad." He turned to Skye in concern. "What'll you do for a maid of honor?"

Her list of woman friends was slim. "Most of my friends at the airport were men. And I had so little time for socializing. I don't know."

Darrick turned a firm gaze on his sister. "Dori'll do it for you. Won't you, Dori?"

"Sure," she said with all the enthusiasm of someone agreeing to skydive without a parachute.

Darrick patted Dori's hand. "That a girl."

"THE SIDE OF THE BED with the phone is mine," Darrick said.

It was after ten, and the twins had been fed and held and put to sleep again. Dori had cleaned up the kitchen, then excused herself to work in her room.

Skye was hanging up her clothes in the closet, and Darrick had just come out of the shower wearing dark blue pajama bottoms. His broad, naked shoulders caught her gaze and led it across a nicely muscled chest lightly dusted with dark hair and down to a tapered waist.

Skye stared at him, her pulse ticking madly, a

hanger with beige cotton pants on it still held in her hand. She was nervous, which was silly, considering they'd just agreed that sex wasn't an option for some time.

But she'd relived being held in his arms for eight long months, certain she'd never have that experience again. And there they were, firmly muscled biceps and triceps nicely defined.

For someone unaccustomed to getting what she wanted—emotionally, at least—this was alien territory.

"Fine," she said, trying to sound relaxed. "Then I'll have first go at the shower in the morning because I'm closer."

He went to the bassinet and readjusted blankets. "Still asleep," he said softly, looking down at the twins with a smile. "I can't believe it. You seem to be a calming influence."

"Really?" She went to stand beside him, pleased at that thought. The babies were snuggled together, Michelle with her tiny hands under her chin, Gabrielle with one hand under the blanket and the other little fist over her eye. Skye tucked that hand under the blanket, too. "Aren't they just such a…miracle?"

"Yes," he agreed. "They are." Then he put an arm around her shoulders and turned her toward the bathroom. "Get ready for bed so we can get some sleep before they wake up again."

"Right."

Skye went to one of the top drawers Darrick had cleared for her in the dresser and pulled out the man's white T-shirt that she always wore to bed.

She changed in the elegant master bathroom, looking forward to a soak in the morning in the sunken tub. It was placed under a frosted window that guaranteed privacy but let in moonlight.

She brushed her teeth, combed her hair, then put both hands over her face as she was attacked by a case of the jitters.

'This is ridiculous,' she told herself again. *'All you're going to do is share the bed with him. What are you so afraid of?'*

And then it occurred to her.

The night after the crash when they'd made love, she'd felt as though he'd discovered something in her even she hadn't known was there. Everything had changed for her because of his tenderness and his astute awareness of everything she needed—emotional and physical.

And she had the most alarming feeling that when he made love to her again, he would be able to read her as well as he had the first time.

Her heart began to beat more rapidly at the thought.

She drew a breath, looked at her reflection frankly and decided that she was an optimist about life, if not about love.

She walked out of the bathroom and into the shadowy bedroom where only the lamp on her bedside table remained lit.

Darrick held the blankets up invitingly. "Glamorous nightwear," he said with a grin.

She climbed in beside him and he pulled the blankets up over her.

"Flannel gets too warm," she explained just for something to say, her voice a little too frail and high as he drew her close to him. "Lace scratches, ruffles bunch up, pajama bottoms get all twisted up…"

"Why don't you just sleep naked?" he asked practically, pulling her into his shoulder and tucking the blankets in over her.

She tried to think of a good answer but it was difficult to come up with even a bad one when her cheek was resting on his warm, solid shoulder and he drew her arm across the sturdy jut of his ribs and placed his own arm over hers. His other hand held her closely to him. She was literally enfolded by him and the comforting warmth of the moment filled her awareness.

"Stretch...marks," she said finally as a delicious drowsiness began to dissolve all her concerns and draw her toward sleep.

His soft laugh was the last thing she heard before she drifted off.

Chapter Five

"I've changed my mind. Why couldn't we just live together? Then we wouldn't *need* blood tests." Skye remained firmly in the passenger seat of Darrick's white Lexus while he held the door open, waiting for her to come out.

He leaned an elbow on the top of the door. He looked fresh and wonderful this morning in jeans and a blue flannel shirt. It was impossible to tell by looking at him that they'd been up with the twins three times. "But getting married was your idea," he said reasonably. "You said it would be better for the babies. Security and all that stuff."

She fiddled with the strap of the purse in her lap. "Yeah, well maybe when they can do a blood test by giving you a pill, I'll feel enthusiastic about it again."

"Ah." He squatted down on the pavement beside her and looked up into her face. His was kind and indulgent. "You're afraid of needles."

She concentrated on her purse. "Yes."

He was silent for a moment, then he put a hand to her stockinged knee just visible under a denim skirt. "Skye, think about this," he said quietly. "When you crash-landed the plane, you were very brave, and at that moment you could have lost your life. Getting blood drawn will only pinch.''

She gave him a stubborn glance. "I know the fear isn't reasonable. It's just there."

"Something to do with your childhood?"

She made a face. "No. Unless you consider that my parents never took me to the doctor. Sometimes I saw the school nurse, but when we were vaccinated at school, it always took three teachers to hold me down."

The more he heard about her parents, the more he wished for five minutes alone in a room with them.

"I was going to take you to pick out a ring afterward." He rubbed her knee gently. "But if you don't get the blood test then we can't get married and there's no point in the ring, is there?"

The stubborn look became one of injured dignity. "I'm not susceptible to bribery with material things."

"All right." He shifted positions and leaned his forearm on her thigh. "What kind of bribery *are* you susceptible to?"

She was weakening. She didn't want to, but she knew there was no alternative to the blood tests. She couldn't allow her dearest wish in all the world to fall victim to one of her oldest fears.

Besides. Every time they'd gone back to bed after caring for the twins, he'd wrapped her in his arms again, and she doubted that she could live without that luxury, now that she'd discovered it.

She turned to him and touched a hand to his forearm resting on her thigh. "Food usually," she admitted with some reluctance.

He raised an eyebrow, apparently surprised, but

willing to exploit that chink in her resistance. "What kind of food?"

"I've always thought the perfect meal," she said, putting it together in her mind, "would be the Mandarin's Banquet from Ming Ha's in San Francisco, followed by one of the cinnamon rolls from the Mariposa Bakery." She met his gaze. "Instead of that runny white frosting stuff they have this cream cheese icing that's so good you want to rub it all over you."

"All over you," he repeated, his voice sounding distracted, as though he were picturing that. "Really."

She sighed. "Yeah. Except that it's so delicious you really don't want to waste any of it."

"Okay." He seemed to have to make an effort to bring himself back to the moment. "In the mall where the jeweler is, there's also a great Chinese restaurant, and a Panier Par Excellence. I don't know what they put on their cinnamon rolls, but if it's the runny white stuff, we'll make them scrape it off and add the frosting from the carrot cake."

She succumbed to a smile, wondering how she'd gotten along without him all this time.

"I warn you," she said, "that I'll require this combination every couple of weeks."

"You got it."

"Okay."

He stood and offered her his hand.

She took it and swung her legs out of the car. "But if I scream or faint," she bargained as she got to her feet, "you have to promise you won't tell anyone."

"I promise."

She didn't scream and she didn't faint. After the technician took his blood, Darrick stood beside her as she awaited her turn, perched on the gurney. She pressed her face into his shoulder when the technician approached her with the syringe.

His name was Vittorio, and it was clear that he and Darrick were well acquainted.

"It's okay," Vittorio said gently as he straightened her arm. "Whatever Darrick told you about me, it isn't true. I am not going to hurt you. Him, maybe, but not you."

Skye felt Darrick's arm come around her and his lips in her hair.

Vittorio tied the strip of tubing above her elbow, and flicked his finger at the vein. "You'd be surprised how many people are afraid of needles," he went on, rubbing alcohol up and down her inner arm. "Okay, here comes the stick. It'll only take a few seconds."

As she waited for the prick and slide of the needle, Darrick lowered his head to whisper in her ear. "Cashew chicken," he said. "Beef lo mein, shrimp chow yuk, mu shu pork, potstickers…"

"Okay, got it."

Skye turned her head to look at the technician in surprise as he taped a gauze pad in place and bent her arm.

"You're finished?" she asked in disbelief.

He held up the syringe then placed it on his rolling tray. "They don't call me Vampire Vittorio for nothing."

She giggled in delirious relief. "Thank you."

He handed her a Tootsie Pop. "No problem. You were an excellent patient." He smiled from her to Darrick. "So, you're getting married. Does Dillon know?"

Darrick shook his head. "It was a sudden decision. You guys heard from him?"

Vittorio shook his head. "That area is pretty remote. And if there was even more damage from the quake than was sustained in Matagalpa, it'll probably still be weeks."

Vittorio's pager beeped. "Gotta go," he said. "If I hear anything, I'll call you."

"Thanks."

Skye leaped off the gurney and pulled down the cuffed sleeve of her blouse.

Darrick caught her other arm as she reached for her purse. "Maybe you should sit a minute," he suggested. "You're a little pale."

She smiled brightly. "I'm strong as a horse. The pallor isn't from weakness but leftover fear. Come on." She took his arm. "We can't leave Dori alone too long, and you owe me Chinese food and a cinnamon roll."

Darrick discovered that Skye did not shop as most other women did. He'd accompanied his mother on marathon shopping expeditions, he'd been with Dori a couple of times, and, once or twice, he'd been forced to shop with a woman he was seeing.

He'd learned that their m.o. was to memorize the entire inventory of every shop in the mall.

But Skye ignored clothing stores, housewares shops, furniture stores and gift boutiques. She stopped at pet shops, Toy Town, wandered in and out of an art display set up in the middle of the mall and seemed fascinated by a suit of armor set up in front of a knife maker's shop.

She read the inscription on the stand that said the armor was an authentic "pucker suit" from fifteenth century Germany.

She walked around it, frowning. "The knight wasn't

very tall, was he?" She patted the exaggerated roundness of the hips and smiled at Darrick. "Must have liked his ale."

He laughed. "I think they wore a lot of stuff under the armor that took up room."

She studied the visor, the articulated shoulder piece, the disks of armor at each armpit obviously intended to protect a raised arm.

"Maybe he was just older," she speculated. "With a wife and children waiting for him to come home."

Then she noticed a jagged rent in the chest plate partially obscured by one of the many "pleats" in the armor for which the pucker suit was named.

"Oh, no," she said, leaning forward to inspect it.

"What?" Darrick leaned over her.

"Look." She ran a finger along the tear in the metal. "He must have taken a blow...right to the heart."

He put his hands on her shoulders, surprised by how upset she seemed. "It happened five hundred years ago, Skye," he reminded her gently.

She leaned back into him. "But I was just getting attached to him. What did his wife and children do when he didn't come home?"

Darrick wrapped his arms around her. "The blow wasn't fatal," he said with conviction.

She turned to face him, clearly anxious to believe he had that information on good authority. "How do you know?" she demanded.

"Well, it's easy to figure out." He swept a hand toward the suit. "You have his profile. Small guy, late thirties or early forties with a fondness for his ale. I'm thinking, judging by what good shape the armor's in otherwise, that his wife kept it polished and cared for, which suggests she loved him very much.''

''Yeah.'' She was warming to his story.

''Well,'' he went on, looking into the hopeful blue of her eyes and feeling himself getting lost in them, ''if he'd been away for a long time she probably had trouble with the castle, trouble with the fields and trouble with the kids.''

Her expression grew worried. ''Yeah.''

''So she wrote him all about it,'' Darrick went on. ''Pages and pages of that tough old parchment paper. Maybe even included a drawing by one of the kids. I think he got the letter the day before the battle, put it in this leather pouch thing in which he kept his treasures, and wore it right over his heart, between him and his armor. I bet the lance stopped somewhere between her tale of the faulty drawbridge and eight-year-old Godwin's fisticuffs with a neighbor boy.''

Her expression changed from concern to happiness very slowly, like a flower opening. And all the time her eyes were looking into his with a warm affection that made him feel boneless.

Then she looped her arms around his neck and rose on tiptoe to give him a long, heartfelt kiss.

He hated to question it, but he had to ask. ''What was that for?''

She kissed him again, quickly this time, and tucked her arm in his. ''For making me believe that that's what happened. Come on. I'm famished!''

She ate heartily, insisting that he try dishes in her combination and picking a shrimp and a piece of egg roll from his.

''Pedestrian stuff,'' she said, indicating his very ordinary and all-fried platter of food.

"You're eating from it," he pointed out.

She smiled. "Just to be polite. It's a custom of the Chinese warlords to eat from their host's plate."

She said it seriously, and since he knew absolutely nothing about Chinese warlords, he would have believed her. Until he saw the laughter in her eyes.

"You're lying!" he accused.

She pretended hurt feelings. "I'm fabricating. Like you did with Godwin's mother's letters. It *could* have been a custom."

When they'd finished lunch, he took her to the jewelry store. She pulled him away from a perusal of diamonds to a showcase of simple bands.

When he saw where she was taking him, he pulled her back.

"All I want," she said stubbornly, "is a plain gold band."

"Fine," he said, spotting a wide filigreed band with a single two-carat solitaire. He pointed to it. "How about that one?"

She leaned in to look, then huffed at him impatiently. "You're not listening to me," she complained quietly as a smiling clerk came toward them on the other side of the counter.

"I am listening," he replied, "I just don't happen to agree."

"It'll be *my* ring."

"But it'll be a token from *me*."

Darrick pointed to the ring and the clerk was quick to unlock the case and place it on a velvet pad on the counter.

Skye put her hands behind her back.

The clerk studied Darrick in puzzlement.

"It's too big to be a token," she insisted with an

apologetic glance at the clerk. "It's a...a...an international declaration big enough to mobilize armies and put lives on the line."

He nodded, seeing no problem with that. "It expresses what I feel. Would you please give the clerk your hand so we can see how it looks?"

She offered a shaky hand to the clerk, who slipped the ring on her finger. Darrick was relieved that it was a perfect fit. Had sizing been required, he knew he'd have had to listen to more arguments.

It looked wonderful on her long, slender fingers with their short but nicely kept nails.

"Very elegant," the clerk said, then looked her over as she studied the ring. He raised his glance to Darrick as though to say, And so is she.

"What do you think?" Darrick asked her.

"It's beautiful." She braced her left hand against her right and held it up as light splashed off the diamond. She looked up at him. "But it's not..."

He nodded to the clerk who slipped it deftly off her finger before she could protest further and reached under the counter for a box, a bag, and his transaction book.

Darrick gave him his American Express card and the clerk excused himself and disappeared into the back to process the payment.

"If you're going to insist that I have it," she complained with a smile and a punch to his shoulder, "you could at least let me wear it."

"Not till the wedding," he said. "It's a tradition among old German knights and Chinese warlords that brides be given their wedding rings only during a ceremony."

She studied him thoughtfully, a pleat between her

eyebrows. "I can't believe that you're the practical one in your family. Your brothers must be absolutely crazy."

"They are," he agreed with a grin.

"Your poor parents."

"Don't pity them." He drew her close and kissed her temple. "The way I see it, they're responsible."

ACTUALLY, HIS PARENTS did not seem to be suffering at all, Skye noticed an hour later when she and Darrick got home to find two strangers sitting in the middle of the sofa, each holding a baby.

That is, they weren't strangers to Darrick.

"Mom!" he said in mild surprise. "Dad. You run out of gambling money already?" He went to the sofa to lean over a plump, pretty woman probably in her early sixties. She raised her face for his kiss.

Skye stopped in the middle of the living room, suddenly frightened. She'd been told that loving parents could read minds.

"No," Darrick's mother replied, her expression gently censuring. "I got worried about you after that call, just before we left, so I called Salishan where you were supposed to be going on vacation, and they said you'd canceled. So I called the hospital to find out if they could tell me where you'd gone, and you know what they said?"

"What?"

"That you'd taken your babies home." She sighed, going on in an exaggeratedly ordinary tone apparently intended to prod his conscience. "So I asked your father if you'd happened to mention to him that you'd had babies, and he said that you hadn't. So we decided there was a distinct possibility we'd become grand-parents and *someone* had forgotten to tell us."

"Hasn't Dori filled you in?" Darrick asked.

"She said she'd leave that to you," his mother replied. "We told her we'd watch the babies while she took a walk to the library."

Seated beside Darrick's mother was a completely bald man with bright, dark eyes and a pleased smile. He freed an arm from under Gabrielle's feet and held it out to Skye. "Come here," he said. "We don't bite, though Peg, here, will talk your arm off, and that can be a slower, more painful death. I'm Charlie, Darrick's father."

Skye took his hand and sat beside him. It was a father's hand, large and gentle, and she absorbed the magic of how it felt. Her father had seldom touched her. "I'm Skye Fennerty."

"I'm pleased to meet you, Skye. This is my wife, Margaret. Peg to everyone."

Peg leaned forward slightly to look around her husband at Skye. Her expression was a little less open, a little less willing to be understanding and forgiving over what she rightfully considered a slight.

"Please don't blame Darrick," Skye said quickly, sitting on the edge of the sofa so she could focus on both parents. She hesitated just a moment to think clearly. "I never…told him I was pregnant. In fact, after the night of your anniversary party…" She paused and looked at Darrick, who now sat on the other side of his mother. "They do know about the crash?"

He nodded. "Yes. But not the…details."

Skye felt her color rise.

"I presume," Charlie said, "that we're holding the results of those details. Go on."

Skye concentrated on trying to put Darrick in the clear. "Darrick tried to get in touch with me repeatedly, but I'd had...a kind of rotten childhood, and all he'd talked about the night we spent on the mountain was how great his family was." Peg's suspicious expression softened a little. "I'd been so...impressed with him because he'd done everything he could to take care of me, and I was very...attracted to him." She sighed, finding the explanation difficult. "But I didn't think there was any way I'd ever fit in with the rest of you because I'd never known what a loving family was like. So I never called him back."

"Even when you knew you were pregnant?" Peg asked.

She hesitated only a moment. "Particularly when I knew I was pregnant. I knew the kind of man he was. He'd have insisted on being a father to the twins, and I was afraid that would just complicate everybody's lives."

"Then...how did you end up having the babies at Valley Memorial?" Charlie asked.

Skye drew a breath, hoping it would help her relax. "The farther along I got in the pregnancy, the more I began to have second thoughts about my decision. So I went to the hospital, intending just to find Darrick and talk. But he was away at a weekend conference, and the twins decided to object to my taking the long trip for nothing by being born."

"So you were there when Darrick came back," Charlie guessed.

Skye met Darrick's eyes and he gave her a small nod, telling her to let the story go at that. She remembered his earlier promise that his parents and brothers didn't have to know that the babies had been abandoned at the hospital.

But Dori knew, and although Skye didn't believe Dori would reveal the facts to anyone if Darrick asked her not to, Skye thought the safest course of action was to stick as closely as possible to what had actually happened.

"No," she said, finding it difficult to look into Peg's and Charlie's faces. "After I had them and they were so perfect, I decided it would be better for them to be with Darrick and his family than with me."

Peg appeared to be dealing with conflicting feelings of sympathy and condemnation. "But the two of you are together."

Skye looked to Darrick, wondering if he would want to explain. But his expression told her she'd gone beyond what he'd thought they should explain, so she may as well finish.

"Darrick came for me," Skye explained. "I had my plane at a little airport in northern California, and he and Dori and the twins showed up at my hangar. We talked things over and…here we are."

"I proposed," he said, as though determined to make a point of that detail anyway, "and she accepted."

"Well, I should hope so," Peg said feelingly as the baby in her arms began to fuss. "We want these little angels to have everything. Is she hungry?" She shooed at Darrick with a plump hand. "Go get me a bottle. We'll see if I remember how to do this."

Darrick went to the kitchen and returned with two bottles, one he handed to his mother and the other he placed on the coffee table in front of his father. "Gabrielle will be awake in a minute, too, Dad. She's the one with the appetite."

Charlie smiled at him. "So this is the one that takes after *you.*"

Darrick laughed. "Michelle's fussier. Takes after Skye."

"So what's the plan now that the two of you are together?" Charlie asked.

Darrick sat on the edge of the coffee table and put a hand to Gabrielle's blanket and one to Skye's knee. "We were just waiting for you and Mom to come home from Vegas so we can get married. We went for blood tests this morning. I thought we'd have all that done and the license in hand before you got back. So now I guess you'll just have to stay with us for a few days until we can get it all together."

Charlie turned to Peg. "We can do that, can't we? Our return reservations are open-ended."

Peg tried to withhold a smile, but finally succumbed to it. "We can. I just wish we'd known about the wedding. We found a wonderful antique shop in Vegas. We could have brought you a great gift."

Darrick struggled to keep a straight face. "That's okay, Mom. We're just glad you're here."

"I love the settee," Skye said, pointing to it in its ragged splendor several yards away.

"You do?" Peg's smile widened. "I thought it was wonderful. Darrick said he liked it," she added with a disparaging glance at her son, "but I think he was just humoring me."

"No, he wasn't." Skye corrected her gravely. "We were just talking yesterday about looking for the right fabric to recover it."

"Well." Peg looked from Darrick to Skye, clearly

adjusting and reassessing the situation. Then she patted the empty sofa cushion beside her. "Come and sit
here, dear, and tell me all about yourself."

Darrick gave her a wink as she left his father's side
to sit beside his mother.

SKYE DEALT with her concerns over her new life by
dosing herself with a cinnamon roll. She sat in bed
with it at 2:13 a.m., unrolling it bite by bite and
munching on it as she stared with burning eyes at the
opposite wall. Darrick lay sound asleep beside her, an
arm thrown across her stomach as she sat propped
against her pillows.

In the beginning, when Darrick had first come to
see her about the babies and she'd decided to marry
him, it all seemed so fated. So right.

But she'd acted on impulse and emotion and forgotten the ripple effect of normal family life.

Peg and Charlie seemed so pleased that Darrick was
getting married and so delighted by the twins, despite
the way it had all come about. On the one hand, she
felt as though she'd brought a new dimension to their
lives they were clearly thrilled with.

On the other hand, Dori didn't like her, and it was
entirely possible her other brothers wouldn't, either.

Darrick awoke suddenly and raised his head, as
though alerted to some tension or danger. "What's the
matter?" he demanded.

She patted the arm around her. "Nothing," she said,
her voice sounding thick. She cleared her throat. "Everything's fine. Go back to sleep."

He propped up on an elbow and rubbed his eyes.
"What are you doing?" he asked.

"Eating a cinnamon roll."

"In the middle of the night?"

"I'm thinking."

"About what?"

"Oh, you know," she replied lightly. "Vaccinations, reading development, ballet classes, knee pads for volleyball, prom dresses, applications for college…"

"Whoa." He sat up beside her and took the cinnamon roll from her hands. "The sugar's obviously got your brain in overdrive. Skye, except for the vaccinations, we've got a while to worry about all that stuff."

"I know," she said, wiping her hands on a towelette that had been in the bag with the roll. "I thought you'd be pleased. You're the organized type. I was just…planning ahead."

"But you should be resting. You can plan better when you've had some sleep." He popped the last bite of her roll into his mouth. He contemplated her as he chewed and swallowed. "Something else worrying you?"

"No," she lied.

"You won my parents over," he said with a smile. She caught the smile, imagining what the future could be like as a permanent part of the McKeon family. "They're wonderful."

"Yes, they are. You're worried about Dori, then?" She could answer that honestly. "A little."

"Well, don't. I'll talk to her."

"No," she insisted, putting a hand to his chest. It was bare and felt wonderfully warm and solid against her fingertips. She forgot what she'd intended to say.

"I will," he said softly, sensual awareness suddenly crackling between them, "if you don't stop worrying and go to sleep." He took her hand in his and put his lips to her palm. "All right?"

"All right," she agreed, knowing that would earn a place for her head on his shoulder and the comfort of his arms around her.

He kissed her temple. "Everything's going to be fine," he said.

She kissed his throat. "Yes," she replied. "Of course it is."

Chapter Six

Darrick held Skye's trembling left hand in his and slipped the much-disputed diamond on her third finger. He repeated the age-old promises, then clasped his hands in front of him and waited for Skye to repeat her vows.

She wore a simple ivory suit she'd shopped for with his mother and Dori the day before, and her dark hair was piled atop her head and woven with baby's breath and pink roses.

His father and Dori stood beside them, serving as witnesses, and his mother watched from behind them with the twins in a carrier.

He was surprised when Skye took his hand and produced a ring. He hadn't purchased one for himself when he'd bought hers, and she hadn't mentioned that she'd shopped for one herself.

But she held his hand in her cool one and slipped a simple gold band on his finger. He looked from it to her and caught the genuine emotion in her eyes as she vowed to love and honor him as long as she lived.

And that was the moment he realized that his life had changed irrevocably.

The babies had changed his routine and brought

about all manner of adjustments in his day to day existence. But Skye had changed his life. He was no longer the solitary man who did his job, loved his parents and his siblings and went his way in pursuit of nothing more than a good round of golf.

Life seemed bigger suddenly, deeper, broader, brighter. It had reaches he hadn't imagined, paths that beckoned, heights he wanted to explore. And all because he suddenly had a soul mate.

The ceremony was over in ten minutes. Dori handed them a large bag of birdseed on the courthouse steps.

Darrick raised an eyebrow. "Thank you," he said, "but isn't this supposed to be tossed at us?"

She nodded. "I just thought as the traditional ritual to guarantee fertility, it was unnecessary." She pointed to the carrier her mother still held. "But I didn't want to bring you bad luck by leaving it out altogether. So. There you are. You can put it in the bird feeder in the backyard."

He hugged her. "You are one weird little sister," he said, taking the carrier. "But, thank you."

"Let's open the bag," his father teased, pretending to reach for it. "They might want more than two children."

Darrick passed the bag off to Skye. "If we do, Dad," he said, "we'll shower ourselves with it. Get in the car. We have lunch reservations downtown."

The top floor of Edenfield's tallest hotel looked out on the busy suburb, office complexes, chic factories, apartment complexes and residential areas all interspersed with trees and flowers and an occasional broad expanse of lawn.

Skye looked down on the scene from her place near the window. At the far end of the table, Peg and Charlie played with the twins while Dori escaped to the ladies' room.

"What are you looking for?" Darrick asked as she studied the view.

"Your house." She pointed through the window to the edge of town and the looser pattern of fewer buildings and more trees. "It's out there, isn't it?"

He leaned over her chair, took her finger and moved it slightly to the left. "There. Just before that big patch of green where the Pierson farm is."

"Oh, yes. It amazes me that it can feel so out-in-the-country when this busy town exists just half a mile from your doorstep."

Darrick hooked a thumb behind him to the other side of the restaurant. "If we were sitting over there, you could see Portland sprawling toward the horizon in the other direction and you'd be even more amazed. Oregon's doing its best to protect its countryside."

"Good. Your home's in such a perfect spot." She turned away from the window, and they were suddenly very close, their lips only inches apart. But she didn't draw back, simply studied him in vague surprise. "We're married," she said in quiet wonder. "I'm having trouble digesting that."

He grinned. "Maybe it's just the Caesar salad."

She laughed and elbowed him in the chest. "No, it's the fact that I'm your wife and you're…my husband. Does it feel strange to you?"

He had to admit that it did. "Strange, yes. But right."

"So you feel married?"

"Yes." He held up his left hand with her ring on it. "You gave me a ring that helps the feeling. But why didn't you tell me?"

"Because you told me you didn't have to have one and I didn't want to fight about it." She looked down at the diamond on her finger and added with a dry smile, "We'd already argued enough over mine." She put her right hand over it and held it to her chest. "I am happy to have it. So I wanted you to have one, too."

"I wish your brothers had been able to be here," Peg said, Gabrielle held to her shoulder as she patted her back. "I think they're going to like being uncles."

Charlie held Michelle up to his face, and they stared at each other with concentration.

"Maybe it'll inspire them to stop globe-trotting and settle down," Peg went on. Then she added with sudden inspiration, "We'll have a reception for you when Dillon and Duncan get home."

"I don't think…" Darrick began, but Peg had tuned him out; she was planning. "Your aunts and uncles and cousins will come, and you and Dillon have a lot of friends in common, so we'll invite them."

Charlie cradled Michelle in his arm and grinned at his son. "Don't discourage her. Maybe Duncan will bring Michelle Pfeiffer and Yvette Delacroix. Then I could die a happy man."

Peg frowned at him across the table. "You're going to die an unhappy man when I impale you with my shrimp fork. Duncan will not bring Michelle Pfeiffer."

"How do you know?"

"Because he doesn't know her."

"How do you know?"

"I'm his mother. I know."

"That's a ridiculous answer. He's thirty-seven and he's been jet-setting around the world since he was twenty-two. You have no idea who he knows and who he doesn't know.''

"Even if he did know Michelle Pfeiffer,'' Skye interposed apologetically, "he probably wouldn't bring her to the party.''

Charlie turned his frowning attention on her. "Why not?''

"Because she's married to a television producer.'' Skye smiled and reached across the table to pat his arm. "But I'm sure that's only because she hadn't met you first.''

Charlie leaned back in his chair with a theatrical sigh. "All my dreams shattered…''

"Your head's about to suffer the same fate,'' Peg threatened.

Dori returned to the table and took her place beside her father. "So…is there a honeymoon planned?'' she asked. "I'd like to see the Grand Canyon or maybe Banff and Lake Louise.''

"It isn't customary to take a little sister on a honeymoon.'' Charlie bounced Michelle gently in his arms as she began to fuss.

"But the nanny goes everywhere,'' Dori said, reaching into the diaper bag at her feet and producing a bottle. She handed it to him. As he fed Michelle, Dori smiled up at Darrick. "So, what do you say? Can we go somewhere where I can work on my tan?''

"Don't you have urgent work to do on a dissertation?'' Darrick asked.

She smiled winningly. "I now have a laptop. I can work anywhere. And you still have a couple of weeks off, don't you?''

He did. And he'd been thinking about going to the beach house, but he wasn't sure that would be fair to

Skye. They'd had it painted outside and scrubbed inside, but the interior needed paint desperately.

And there was no furniture yet, not even dishes or pots and pans in the kitchen. That could be taken care of easily enough, but would it be fair to impose less-than-perfect conditions on a new mother of ten-day-old twins?

On the other hand, he was in desperate need of physical activity or he would self-destruct under the influence of a suppressed libido and all the new adjustments in his life.

He could live with the celibacy required of him for the next four and a half weeks, but he needed something to do! Something physical that would tax his strength, require his concentration, and leave him exhausted.

Maybe he should just stay home and put in a pool with a shovel as his only tool.

"If you take babies and a nanny on a honeymoon," Peg said, "you can no longer experience what a honeymoon is supposed to be all about. Intimacy, privacy—" she smiled wistfully "—sowing the seeds of romance that will last a lifetime."

Charlie raised an eyebrow at Darrick. "I thought a honeymoon was about strutting down the boardwalk with a pretty young thing on your arm, then making sure you didn't come home with a tan—even in August."

Peg made a face at him. "That's why our romance lasted only until the Tuesday after the wedding."

Darrick shook his head over his parents and turned to Skye, wanting to reassure her that their teasing was just that, but he could see by the fond way she watched them that she understood.

He'd spent a lot of time apart from them since he went away to college, but before that he'd always been aware that they'd had a cheerful and robust affection for one another.

Now they teased each other about age all the time, and it was entirely possible that time and the beginnings of physical limitation had quelled their ardor. But he knew that their love for each other—the deepdown devotion that led them from day to day—was stronger than it had ever been.

Skye caught his glance and smiled at him, sharing the moment.

"You had five children, Mom," Dori pointed out reasonably. "The romance must have lasted longer than that."

Peg fought a smile. "I was just a pushover for flowers. Seems every time he brought me a bouquet, we had a baby nine months later."

Dori patted Charlie's shoulder. "Flowers, Dad? That's very poetic."

"Mmm," Charlie replied. "Good thing I wasn't poetic more than five times over forty years. You guys were a high price to pay for a little romance."

"Oh, come on," Darrick chided. "You adore every one of us. Me, especially."

Dori made a scornful sound. "Why you especially? I'm the cute one."

"I'm the one who takes him fishing."

"Well, if I wanted to murder helpless fish, I could take him fishing, too."

The cheerful banter ended abruptly when Gabrielle objected loudly to some indeterminate problem and began to screech. Skye took her, but the baby resisted all attempts to calm her and soon involved Michelle in the revolution.

Their quiet corner of the restaurant was suddenly in chaos. The party was over.

Charlie snatched the check from Darrick as Darrick reached for his wallet.

"Now, now," Peg soothed, picking up her purse and the empty carrier. "It's the least we can do. You've made us grandparents and you've taken Dori off our hands for an entire summer." She smiled teasingly into her daughter's indignant expression. "We love you, dear, but you inhibit our sex life."

Dori blinked, pretending shock. "You still have one?"

"Of course. And now that we know we can't produce any more of you, it's just fun."

"Really," Charlie added, hooking an arm around Peg's shoulders. "Maybe now we can try that ice-cube gravity boots thing."

Everyone laughed so loudly that the babies stopped crying.

SKYE WAS SURPRISED to find herself choked with emotion when she said goodbye to Darrick's parents the following day. They all stood on the sidewalk in front of the house as Charlie closed the trunk of the rental car on their bags.

"When are you coming back?" Skye asked as she hugged Peg. Darrick held the twins in their carrier.

"In a couple of weeks," Peg replied. "Charlie's birthday is Memorial Day and we always get together to barbecue."

"I was thinking we could do it at the summer house," Darrick said.

His parents and Dori looked at him as though he'd gone mad. Peg put a hand to his forehead.

"Darling, I know the sudden pressures of marriage and fatherhood are difficult, but think—we don't have a summer house."

He took her diagnostic hand, pinched it punitively, then kissed it. "I mean the place Dillon and Duncan and I bought."

"But you said it was a mess."

"Well, I thought Skye and Dori and the girls and I could go down there for a couple of weeks and work on it."

Peg looked horrified. "But you can't ask Skye to live in a bummy old place with two babies while…"

Darrick held his ground, more and more determined this was a good idea. "We'll stay in a motel until I can get at least one room in good shape. I can have most of the rooms painted and the roof fixed by Memorial Day. We'll get a bed in for you two and the rest of us can rough it in sleeping bags." He indicated the carrier he held. "The girls'll be comfortable no matter what."

Peg and Charlie looked at each other. Then Peg grinned. "This is great. Wait'll I tell my poker group we're having your birthday party at our kids' summer place. That has such snob appeal."

Darrick shook his head indulgently. His friends' mothers played bridge. His mother played poker.

Dori shook her head at Darrick. "Didn't they teach us *not* to flaunt what we were privileged to have?"

"Yeah. I guess the rules don't apply to them."

"Bill and Sandra Wentworth are always lording it over us," Peg said, hands on her hips in self-defense, "because *their* two boys have a software company and are always taking them to Aspen for the weekend, or to Paris shopping. Now I'll have something on them.''

"Mom, I know the pressure of grandparenthood can be difficult,'' Darrick said, quoting her, "but think. The cabin isn't in Aspen or Paris. It's in Dancer's Beach, Oregon—population 2,021. Even though Dunk and Dill and I fell in love with it, it'll never compare with the Wentworths' jaunts so I wouldn't try to lord it over them with it, okay? Because the day will come when they'll ask to see your photos.''

Peg patted his cheek. "We'll show them pictures of the twins.'' She reached into her large purse and produced the disposable camera with which she'd taken photos of the babies and of him and Skye dressed for their wedding. She grinned with vindictive relish. "Her boys are so busy making money, they don't have time to make babies. So we're two up on them already. And I'm going to enjoy rubbing it in.''

After hugs and handshakes, Darrick, Skye and Dori stood at the curb and watched the senior McKeons drive away.

"Do you ever wish,'' Dori asked Darrick moodily as she watched the car diminish into a tiny dot, "that we were all in the furniture business, or that we had a grocery store or something?''

Darrick turned to her in surprise. "Why?''

She jammed her hands into the pockets of baggy slacks still staring at the spot where the dot had disappeared. "Because we'd all always be here. Mom and Dad wouldn't have to leave to go home, they could just walk down the street or something. And Duncan wouldn't always be in Hollywood or New York or wherever, and Dillon wouldn't be chasing disasters around the globe.''

Darrick set the carrier down on the sidewalk and pulled Dori into his arm. "You expect the McKeons to live conventional lives?" he teased, wondering what had brought about her serious mood. "Never happen, Dori. Mom and Dad will always be too young at heart to settle down near the kids, Duncan needs lights and a camera to play to, and even if we did own a grocery store, Dillon would go to South America to buy the fruit and coffee beans. He's got to be on the move."

Dori leaned into his shoulder and sighed. "So you're telling me that I'm stuck with *you*."

He squeezed her shoulder. "No. *I'm* stuck with me. You're the one who's doing her graduate work in England, remember? Like you'd be any happier selling furniture or fig Newtons than Dill or Dunk would."

"I guess," she admitted grudgingly. She patted his chest, then leaned down to pick up the carrier. "It's just that this is such a great street, and every time I come here, I think how neat it would be if Mom and Dad were across the street, if Dill and Duncan shared a house next door, and maybe...Donovan was still here."

He studied her closely. "You get lonesome in England?"

"Terribly," she admitted, then dismissed her pensive mood with a wave of her free hand. "I always feel very independent and self-sufficient until I see you all again, then I realize how special you all are. But I'm sure I'll come to my senses any minute now. I'll take the girls inside."

Darrick watched her head up the walk and turned to Skye, standing beside him. "Can you imagine my family all together on the same block?"

She laughed lightly. "Well, I've yet to meet your brothers, but I can imagine if your parents lived across the street there'd never be a dull moment or an event unphotographed."

He pretended to shudder and she punched his shoulder. "Stop that. To someone who's longed for family all her life, that sounds like a wonderful idea. And apparently it does to Dori, too."

"Yeah."

"She feels deprived that she didn't know Donovan," Skye observed.

Darrick drew a deep breath. He always thought it remarkable that the memory of a bright-eyed little boy could linger so vividly when he and his brothers had all been so young at the time of his death.

"We're all haunted by Donovan," he said, putting an arm around her. "Duncan lives his life changing identities because he doesn't want to be the big brother who couldn't save him, and Dillon chases all over the world saving other people for the same reason."

Skye leaned into him. "And you?"

He shrugged. "I don't know. It's easier to analyze other people." He led Skye up the walk, then detoured around the house to the backyard where a forsythia bush was in bright yellow bloom, apparently wanting to eliminate himself from the discussion. "Anyway, Dori surprised me with that nostalgic mood. I thought she was loving her independence."

Skye spread her fingers to touch a honeysuckle bush as they passed it. "But her work centers on nineteenth-century novelists with an emphasis on Jane Austen. And her work is full of families who quarrel, but love one another very much, and turbulent relationships that usually have a happy ending. Maybe Dori's already longing for her own happy ending.''

"Ending? She's only twenty-three!"

"Well, we call it a happy *ending* but what it really means is the *beginning* of a long-term relationship. Is she seeing anyone?"

He shrugged a shoulder as he led her to the bird feeder dangling from the bottom branch of an ash tree abloom with white flowers. "We haven't talked about it, but I don't think so. She's always been such a studious little thing, more interested in literary romance than in her own." He tapped the empty feeder. "Hold on. I'll get the bag of seed."

He retrieved the sack from the kitchen, snipped a corner off and, pinching the bag closed, carried it carefully outside. Skye waited under the tree, looking like some sun-dappled woodland fairy peering up into the canopy of leaves and making chirping sounds.

The air was warm and sunny and filled with the delicious fragrances of spring. He took a deep breath of it, feeling intoxicated. But he knew the late-morning air hadn't brought about the whirling in his head. Skye was responsible.

Life would be chugging along at a comfortable pace and he would feel attuned to his place in it, then with the sudden impact of a wall on the tracks she would derail him. She would do or say something that would make him forget everything but the image she presented at that moment.

Now a small, fat chickadee stood on the roof of the empty feeder and Skye held her index finger up to it, trying to coax it down.

Her arm stretched out gracefully like a detail in fine sculpture. Her sun-glossed hair, worn loose this morning, streamed down her back as she reached up, and her laugh drifted musically on the quiet breeze.

She turned when she sensed his approach and took a step back from the feeder to let him fill it. The little chickadee flew away.

"Maybe Dori's realizing she wants more out of life than academic achievement," Skye said. "Maybe she's just…ready."

Darrick pushed the feeder roof back and filled the well with seed. He heard the branches of the tree spread out above him stir with activity. The little chickadee had apparently alerted his family and friends.

Darrick lowered the roof and pulled Skye back to the verdigris bench in the middle of the lawn. They sat together quietly and watched the birds come. The chickadee was first with a twin, then a robin came and a wild canary.

There was chirping and fluttering and a little cloud of husks as seed flew everywhere.

"Aren't they beautiful?" Skye asked in a whisper. "Finding a full feeder is probably like being invited to Buckingham Palace for lunch."

Darrick kept his voice down and leaned toward her. "Do you recognize any of them?"

She raised an eyebrow in question.

"Well, they fly. You fly," he said. "I thought you might know each other."

She giggled. It was a surprising but pleasing sound coming from the same woman he'd seen control a crashing plane.

"No. I don't know them. But I *am* friends with a few blue jays in Mariposa. And there's a pelican I always watch for when I eat at Castangnola's in San

Francisco on my freight runs.'' She smiled warmly at him and he felt his pulse accelerate madly. "How about you? Any bird friends?"

"Just the stork that brought my babies,'' he answered softly, lowering his head toward hers. He had to kiss her. He couldn't fight it.

Her lips met his, warm and supple like the breeze that swirled around them. They shared their pleasure in the morning, their interest in each other, the simple wonder of lives caught in a sweet space of time.

Darrick finally drew away on the brink of deepening the kiss. Their feelings had to be confined to the limits of an embrace, and he faced that reality with reluctant acceptance.

"How would you feel about a couple of weeks at the beach?" he asked, brushing her hair out of her face as the breeze drew it across her eyes. "Frankly, it isn't the most comfortable place in the whole world right now, but there's a posh hotel where you and the girls can spend the first few days until I get a room cleaned and painted."

She frowned over that suggestion and he thought she was about to reject the idea. "Well…just how bad is it?" she asked.

"My brothers and I bought it a couple of months ago," he answered, "thinking it'd be a good base for summer vacations. Dillon and Duncan crave the quiet, and you do get that in Dancer's Beach. And I like to golf and fish, and there's a great course just a few miles down the coast and a wonderful stream filled with steelhead about half a mile inland. It's a perfect spot."

She seemed to drink in his words, as though imagining his and his brothers' pleasure in the place.

"Anyway," he went on, "it had been empty for about a year, and everything was dusty and musty. We had the exterior painted, and a cleaning service came in to scrub walls and cupboards because Dill thought he'd be right back. Then something came up in Mexico, and he was off. He went straight from there to Nicaragua."

"So, it's been cleaned fairly recently."

"Yeah, but the inside's all yellow and lavender."

She blinked. "Together?"

"No. But all the rooms that aren't lavender are yellow. It's pretty awful."

"But it's clean."

"Well, that was about two months ago."

She shook her head over that detail. "I'd like to go if I don't have to sit in a hotel room. I'm very good with a paintbrush."

"You've got the twins," he reminded her.

She looked him in the eye. "*We* have the twins," she said, "and I'll help you with the cleaning and painting if you'll help me with them."

"But should you be stretching and reaching so soon after delivering?"

"I'm in great shape. The sea air would probably be good for all of us. But what do you think Dori will say if we take her away from the library? I don't imagine a town of two thousand will have a large enough library to accommodate her research."

He leaned an elbow on the back of the bench. "I thought about that. I even considered telling her she could stay home and have a couple of weeks to herself while we spend that time getting better acquainted." He frowned, remembering his sister's nostalgic thoughts as their parents drove away. "But she sounded so melancholy this morning, I don't want her to feel rejected or displaced.''

"So, we'll take her along if she wants to come,'' Skye said simply.

He studied her in consternation. "Are you always so agreeable? I'm beginning to believe that you're just too good to be true. Tell me I'm not going to wake up in the morning and discover that you're a figment of my imagination.''

Her eyes widened and grew dark, and for an instant he couldn't make sense of that. Then she laughed, and he realized it was just a trick of the shadow on her face caused by the comb-shaped leaves of the ash tree overhead.

"Yes, I am,'' she said, fluffing her hair in a show of theatrical self-importance. "And I'm pleased to see that you appreciate me. I presume this means that while we're at the beach, I can trust you not to ogle other women in swimsuits?''

"You can trust me not to touch,'' he said, getting to his feet and offering her a hand to help her to hers. "But ogling's another matter.''

"No, it's not.'' She followed as he led her across the yard toward the back door. She loved the feel of his large hand surrounding hers. "You're married now, remember.''

He held the door open for her and pretended a frown. "But you just told me that you're always agreeable.''

"I am,'' she said. "But sometimes I'm also a liar.''

Chapter Seven

Skye studied the sorry contents of her side of the wardrobe closet.

"I don't have much in the way of beach wear," she said, looking through the sturdy slacks, jeans and shirts she'd worn around the airport, and the single woolen dress she owned for the rare occasions in her life that called for one. "But I do have the market cornered on clothes to clean and paint in."

"The weather on the Oregon beach is still pretty cool in May." Darrick carried a pile of T-shirts and socks to the suitcase open in the middle of the bed. "But we can buy you whatever else you need when we get there."

Skye grinned and pointed to the stack of baby things piled in a corner. It was enough to outfit an entire nursery—twice.

"There won't be room for our stuff in the car, anyway," she said. "I'll have to sit in a U-haul trailer attached to the hitch."

"I'll find room for you," he assured her, adding several sweatshirts to the suitcase. He straightened, hands on his hips, to eye her slender bottom in a pair of jeans. "I thought regaining your figure was supposed to be an ordeal for women—particularly after twins.''

"I...was in good shape." She'd used that explanation before. "It doesn't take long to get it back.''

"But you look like Cindy Crawford and it's only been ten days. In fact, you were trim when I found you just a few days after the twins were born.''

She shook her head. "How could you tell? I was wearing a jumpsuit that hid everything. You were so glad to find someone to help you with the twins that you just *thought* I looked good.''

He covered the small distance between them, hooked an arm around her waist and pulled her into his arm. "I *was* glad to find you. I expected to have to chase all over creation for you, but there you were, just like I remembered you. Geez." He buried his face in her hair. "This is going to be the longest four weeks of my life.''

She held him tightly, wanting to make love with him as desperately as he wanted her. "I know," she whispered. "Mine, too.''

The doorbell peeled loudly downstairs.

"Want me to get it?" Skye kissed his cheek and tried to push out of his arms.

But he tightened his grip on her. "No, I don't want you to move. Dori'll get it.''

He ran a splayed hand gently up and down her spine, pausing at her hip to fill his hand with her, then moving up again.

She went weak with longing, leaning into him even farther, relishing the muscled firmness of his embrace.

"Darrick!" Dori called. "Come see who's here!''

Darrick raised his head and looked into Skye's eyes, his own turbulent with unresolved desire.

"I don't suppose it would be cool to tell her I don't care who's here?"

"Definitely not," Skye replied, giving him a quick kiss and pulling out of his arms. "Lust is not an excuse to forget your manners."

"It's Harper!" Dori's voice shouted, high with apparent delight.

Darrick smiled widely. "All *right*," he said, and pulled Skye with him as he headed for the stairs.

Skye hurried to keep up. "Who is he?"

"He's a she," Darrick replied under his breath as they started down the carpeted stairs. "Dillon's old girlfriend. You'll like her."

If she hadn't had that assurance, Skye thought as Darrick introduced them, she might have hated Harper Harriman on sight. The woman was everything Skye had ever wanted to be—small, blond, beautiful and confident.

Her almost-platinum hair was worn in a short, puffy little do that enhanced the shape of her heart-shaped face. She wore little gold hoops at her ears and casual yellow slacks topped by a matching long-sleeved yellow shirt.

She was leaning over the bassinet, and in her arms were two very large teddy bears. She straightened as Darrick and Skye walked into the room.

"My God, it's true!" she said, hazel eyes bright with astonishment. "One of my classmates from high school is a nurse at Valley Memorial and she told me…" She paused to shake her head in amazement. "Darrick! You're a father!"

Darrick took one of the bears from her and wrapped her in his free arm. "It's great to see you Harp. How are you? What brings you to Edenfield?"

"I came home for a couple of months to keep an eye on Aunt Phyl." She cast a smiling glance at Skye. "She had knee replacement surgery, so I left my partner in charge of the studio and came down to be a sort of nurse-housekeeper for a couple of months."

"Lucky for us," Darrick said, putting a hand to Skye's back and urging her forward. "Skye, I'd like you to meet Harper Harriman. She has a photo studio in Seattle. Harper, my wife, Skye. Remember the airplane crash that delayed my arrival to the anniversary party last year?"

Harper took Skye's hand, looking puzzled. "Yes, I do."

"Skye was my pilot."

"You're kidding!"

Skye frowned at Darrick. "That was a lovely introduction. Now she's probably afraid of me."

Harper laughed and squeezed her hand. "Not at all. I've always thought a crash of some kind would serve all the McKeon boys well. I just didn't have a plane to do it in. Good for you."

"But I didn't do it on purpose."

"Well, you should have."

Remembering suddenly that she was the hostess here, Skye gestured her to the sofa. "Please sit down. Can I get you something to drink? We have coffee, tea, Pepsi, formula."

"A cup of coffee would be wonderful."

Skye prepared a pot of the richly aromatic Perugia blend that Darrick preferred, her ear attuned to the cheerful conversation in the other room.

Darrick had said Harper was Dillon's *old* girlfriend. That information along with Harper's wicked glance when she'd said she'd thought a crash would do all the McKeon boys good made Skye wonder just what had brought about the end of Harper's relationship with Dillon.

Whatever it was, it probably hadn't been amicable. Though it was clear Dillon's family was fond of Harper and she of them.

It would be hard, she thought, to have been on the inside of this family and then find yourself out.

She put cookies on a plate, cups on a tray and carried it all out to the living room.

"But…I can't leave you alone," Dori was saying to Darrick as Skye placed the tray on the coffee table. Dori and Harper sat on opposite sides of the sofa. Darrick sat on the decrepit Gothic love seat.

"Skye and I can manage," Darrick said. "We're going to the beach house, anyway."

Dori's cheeks were pink, her eyes bright. "But I'd be gone four days. What if you want to go out, or if you just need a break? I mean the babies have kept all three of us up all night a couple of times. What'll you—"

"Hey," he said, catching Skye's hand and pulling her into his lap. "The twins are *our* life sentence, not yours. You can have four days off, Dori. Can't she, Skye?"

"Of course." Skye hooked an arm around his neck, liking the possessive way he laced his fingers around her. "But where's she going?"

"To Boston with Harper, who's also getting a few days' reprieve from her duties with her aunt. She's going to a conference on Victorian art and she thought Dori might find something useful in it for her thesis."

"I've had the tickets for months," Harper said, sugaring a cup of coffee. "My partner was going to join me, but something came up for him.'' She rolled her eyes. ''He has a very turbulent love life. So I was just going to pass on the whole thing, too, then my aunt's friend came to visit and insisted I take a break. Now I have an extra ticket.''

Skye thought about a few days alone with Darrick, except for the twins. That both delighted and alarmed her. But she smiled assurance at Dori.

''It sounds like great fun. Darrick and I will be fine. Go and have a good time.''

''You're just anxious to get rid of me.'' Dori's expression was half teasing, half accusing.

Certain a sweetly phrased denial would sound false, Skye leaned an elbow on Darrick's shoulder and nodded. ''Yes, I am, but please don't let that get in the way of your having a good time.''

Harper laughed a little uncertainly, but Skye thought she saw the first flicker of respect in Dori's eyes.

''I'm leaving the day after tomorrow,'' Harper prodded. ''What do you say, Dori?''

Dori focused on Darrick and Skye. ''You're *sure?*''

Skye nodded.

''Positive,'' Darrick said.

''And I don't have to give the laptop back?''

''Yes, you do.''

Skye put a hand over his mouth. ''Don't listen to him,'' she said to Dori. ''Just go and learn great stuff and have a wonderful time.''

Harper asked about Darrick's and Dori's parents, then after half an hour or so of reminiscences, went to the bassinet to have another look at the babies.

She put a fingertip to their little hands, joined as they often were on top of their blankets, and shook her head wistfully. Skye thought she saw her draw a ragged breath before she straightened to give Darrick a last hug.

"Just in case I don't see you again before I go back to Seattle," she said. She hugged Skye. "I wish you and your babies all good things. And if you talk this guy into bringing you to Seattle, I'll take a family portrait for you."

"That'd be wonderful," Skye said. "I'd love to see your studio."

Harper pointed to Dori. "I'll pick you up six-thirty Thursday morning."

"I'll be ready," Dori replied.

They followed Harper across the lawn to the driveway where her car was parked behind Darrick's.

"Any messages for Dillon?" Darrick asked quietly.

Harper looked at him, her jaw firm, but her eyes wide and uncertain. Then she drew a sigh and said, "Nothing repeatable. Take care, all."

Darrick went back upstairs to finish packing while Skye carried the dishes into the kitchen and put them in the dishwasher.

Dori cleaned out the coffeepot and wiped off the counters. "You're sure you'll be okay," she asked Skye, the tone of her voice intended to convey little interest in the answer.

"We'll be fine." Skye put the creamer in the refrigerator and pretended the same disinterest.

"You'll be all alone."

"Hardly. I'll be with Darrick."

"But he'll be painting. Most of the time, you'll have to deal with the little angels all by yourself." Dori tossed the sponge in the sink and turned her attention on Skye. "You're already down to about four hours sleep a night and that's *with* me trying to help you."

"I've appreciated your help." Skye met her gaze and held it. "But that's what I'm supposed to do. It's my job. You, on the other hand, as the nanny, are entitled to a week off. So please don't think any more about it. When you come back, you're welcome to join us at the beach if you want to, or if you'd rather stay here and work until we get back, that'd be fine, too."

Dori studied her soberly for a moment, as though unable to make up her mind about her.

Skye stared back intrepidly, an affection developing for her sister-in-law-nanny, who was always on the job.

Dori finally nodded. "Okay. You want to borrow some clothes to take to the beach? You're taller, but I have a couple of pairs of shorts where the length of the leg wouldn't matter. And I have some long T-shirts that should be just right on you."

Skye did her best to conceal the surprise and pleasure she felt at the friendly offer.

"I do need some things," she said. "Thank you."

Darrick was distracted some time later from a search under the bed for a second tennis shoe by the sound of feminine laughter across the hall. He straightened from a crouch to listen.

There was a high, slightly hectic laugh—Dori's. Then a lower, throaty laugh. Skye's. Neither was unusual, but he was hearing them together. After witnessing a week of cool politeness between them, he had to make sure that what he heard wasn't some bizarre manifestation of frayed tempers finally snapping.

He was comforted a moment later by the certainty that this hilarity had nothing to do with tempers and everything to do with a bikini lying in the middle of

Dori's bed. The bra and panties looked like some salesman's miniature sample.

"I swear it's true," Dori said as the laughter abated. She was propped against her pillows and Skye sat at the foot of the bed, leaning against one of the posts. "I won it in a game of Trivial Pursuit. There was this girl in our flat from Dorchester. A biology major with a passion for research, if you know what I mean."

The two women erupted into laughter again. After a moment, Dori continued. "And she was very smart. Her father's in the House of Lords. So her question was, what was the name of Alexander the Great's horse. And she didn't know!"

Skye rolled her eyes theatrically. "Such appalling ignorance." Then she cocked an eyebrow. "What *is* the name of Alexander the Great's horse?"

"Bucephalus," Dori said, picking up the top of the bikini and studying it with a sudden frown. "I've known that since I was twelve." She sighed forlornly and dropped the bikini bra. "Men don't like brains, you know. Even smart men. They still want to be superior to you even when it's brains and not brawn or beauty involved. And if you're not willing to fake it, they go looking for some pretty little thing who doesn't have to."

Darrick leaned a shoulder in the doorway, still unnoticed. This was a problem for which he'd provided a shoulder to Dori on several occasions. His insistence that one day she would find a man who'd be delighted by her brain hadn't helped.

"Well, you know…" Skye said, picking up the bra, "you may not like the rules of the world, but sometimes to get along you have to play by them, anyway."

Dori blinked at her. "What do you mean?"

Yeah, Darrick thought. What do you mean?

"Having a skill that's usually a male province," Skye explained, pulling on the stretchy fabric, "like flying a plane, means that a woman is treated in the same way you're describing. So, sometimes to get their attention, you have to make the packaging as attractive as the contents."

Dori bristled. "I hate that kind of sexism."

Skye nodded emphatically. "Me, too. But if you're ever going to get the chance to make them appreciate what you can do, you have to get their attention. And, frankly, when you first meet a man, his reactions are mostly glandular."

"You're saying we have to play down our brains and our talents?"

"Absolutely not. But we may have to play up our physical appeal."

"But all that gets you," Dori argued, "is the kind of man who judges a woman on looks."

"They all judge on looks," Skye countered, "but the discerning ones eventually notice wit, personality, and intelligence—if you maintain their interest long enough."

"Do they ever respect those things about you?"

"Yes." Darrick walked into the room with a frown of disapproval for his wife and his sister. "But do women ever notice that some men are very civilized and don't operate on a strictly glandular level? That you can't tar us all with the same brush?"

Skye stretched a hand out for his and drew him toward her. "But you are all the same when a man and woman first meet."

"I wasn't," he insisted.

She laughed. "You and I are hardly the classic case,

Darrick. I stranded you with me on top of a mountain with no way out until help arrived. You couldn't have walked away from me if you'd wanted to."

"Maybe," he granted, "but I didn't have to share my box of Raisinettes with you, did I? Or my superior wood-gathering skills."

"True, but that just proves you're a gentleman. Not that you'd have given me a second thought had we not crashed."

"Skye," Dori said, sitting up cross-legged as though suddenly aware of new information. "You're missing something important here."

"What?" Skye asked.

"Not only did you pilot the plane Darrick flew in, but you managed to land it in relative safety and save his life. So if he had reacted like the typical male we're talking about, he should have wanted to get as far away from you as he could."

"But we were stranded on a mountaintop."

Dori shook her head. "He kept calling you from Mom and Dad's," she said. "I stayed for an extra couple of days, and I saw him call you repeatedly and leave messages."

Skye remembered what it had felt like to hear his voice. At a time when she'd been unutterably lonely, it had brought back all the warmth of that night. But it also reminded her that Tommy had claimed to love her then left her.

"You're the one who didn't return *his* calls." Dori hammered her with the details. "So…maybe he's the only exception to your rule, but he is an exception."

Darrick inclined his head modestly. "Thank you, Sis." He arched an eyebrow at Skye.

"Okay, I'm sorry," she said, getting to her feet. "I

lost my head. There's nothing typical about you. I was in error when I tarred you with the glandular-male brush.''

He'd folded his arms, and his weight rested on one hip as he considered her apology. He did not appear satisfied. ''That's the best you can do?'' he asked.

Skye met Dori's amused gaze. ''I think it's time for us to say good-night.'' She handed back the bikini bra. ''Put that in your suitcase,'' she said. ''There might be a pool where you and Harper are staying. And thanks for the loan of the shorts and T-shirts.'' She picked up the neat pile of clothes on the chair.

''You're welcome.'' Dori climbed off the bed and went to hold her bedroom door open for them. ''I'm going to work for a while tonight, so if I'm not up when you leave in the morning, have a great time. I'll call you when I get back to see if you need me to come down there or what.''

''Okay.'' Darrick hugged her. ''You have a great time, too. And be careful where you aim that bikini.''

''Don't worry. I'll be with Harper, and she says she's been off men since Dillon, so I doubt I'll even get within yards of eligible men. Good night.''

In the bedroom, Skye placed the T-shirts and shorts in the suitcase open on the bed beside Darrick's, then she went to the bassinet to check Michelle and Gabrielle. They remained fast asleep, little bodies snuggled into each other.

She took a moment to admire the miracle of their perfect little faces. Then she applied herself to the little game she and Darrick played of trying to find some difference in their features that would distinguish one from the other. But it was futile. They were as identical as if one had been cloned from the other.

"Stop admiring your work," Darrick said, "and see what you can do about improving upon that apology." He closed the suitcases as he spoke and placed them on the floor near the baby things. "I'm still wounded that you would lump me in with all other men."

She came to wrap her arms around his waist and smile up into his eyes. "Especially because of the Raisinettes?"

"Yes," he replied gravely. "In moments of stress, they're like a tranquilizer to me. And I *shared* them with you."

She rested her forehead on his shoulder in a show of abject repentance. "How could I have been so wrong?" She looked up at him again, dropping the repentance and pinning him with a knowing look. "Unless it's the fact that earlier tonight when we were talking about seeing each other again for the first time in eight months in my hangar in Mariposa, you said I'd looked slender in my jumpsuit. Not that I looked smart or charming or bright—but slender. You noticed my body, not *me*."

He returned her firm gaze. "You can't detect charm or brilliance by appearance—at least not right away."

"My point exactly," she replied. "But if I'd grown fat and funny looking, would you have accepted my proposal?"

"Of course."

"Why?"

He framed her face in his hands and leaned over her with sudden and complete concentration. "Because that plane crash was no accident," he said. She saw humor deep in his eyes, but over it were lust and affection and confused surprise all inextricably entangled. He loved her, she realized with sudden insight and wonder, and he was mystified by that knowledge.

"We were struck by some celestial lightning bolt," he went on fancifully. "Our union was a cosmic decree. A fate plotted eons ago and finally brought to fruition on that mountaintop." He kissed her fervently, lengthily, then he raised his head and focused on her again. "We were meant to be, Skye."

She stared into his eyes and drank in that conclusion. Meant to be. Meant to be.

She held on as he lifted her into his arms. The two weeks in Dancer's Beach were a gift to her, she knew. She and Darrick would be alone together, except for the babies, and it would be her chance to convince him that he'd made a smart move in marrying her.

She was good with the babies, and growing a little more comfortable and more knowledgeable every day. He appreciated that in her; she could see it in his eyes.

Now she could prove to him that she was handy with a scrub brush or a paintbrush, that she could be happy in less-than-perfect conditions and do her share to improve them, and that while she didn't believe any woman ever had to devote her life to catering to a man, nurturing was in her nature. She would take pleasure in anticipating Darrick's needs and filling them.

This could all come out beautifully if she applied herself.

Darrick placed her in the middle of the bed and drew the other side of the bedspread over her. "Rest," he said. "I'm going to take a shower."

Skye drifted off to sleep on the thought of how nice it would have been if she'd been able to shower with him.

Chapter Eight

"Where did the name Dancer's Beach come from?" Skye asked.

They'd completed the winding drive from the valley to the coast, and were now headed south on Highway 101, the girls sleeping contentedly in their infant seats in the back. The day was rainy and cool, and Skye had had to pull a sweatshirt on over one of Dori's T-shirts, but she was filled with the excitement of the first day of a vacation.

Not that she'd ever had that experience herself. When she'd been a child there'd never been money for vacations, nor any eagerness on her parents' parts to spend time together in an intimate hideaway.

She'd seen movies, though, *Mr. Hobbs Takes a Vacation, Houseboat, Two for the Road.* In each case the vacation had caused the families emotional turbulence, which had eventually been overcome by their love for one another.

"According to the probably romanticized brochure put out by the Chamber of Commerce," Darrick answered her, pausing to concentrate as he negotiated a hairpin turn. There was a rock wall on the inland side and a considerable drop to the surf on the right. Skye noted that without nervousness as Darrick drove with confidence-inspiring ease.

The road straightened a short distance ahead and he continued. "It was settled in 1890-something when four dance-hall girls headed for the Klondike were shipwrecked off the coast."

Skye turned toward Darrick, fascinated by the story. "How did they save themselves?" She pointed toward the ocean strewn with picturesque but lethal rocks. "It must be treacherous out there."

"To say the least." He sent her a quick, smiling glance. "You'll love this part. There were three brothers who worked a small mill just off the coast, and one of them was on a hill covered with fir trees, considering it for a spot on which to put up their new home, and saw the ship run aground. He collected his brothers and a couple of neighbors and they managed to save all the dancers and most of the crew."

She did love it. "Please tell me the brothers married the dancers."

"They did. Well, three of them. I don't know what happened to the fourth dancer." He laughed. "I think that's part of what appealed to Dillon and Duncan and me. As kids we used to think it'd be great to be in business together, but we grew up with vastly different interests and personalities, and though we generally get along well, I don't think we could come up with a business we could all enjoy. But it was cool that the Buckley brothers did."

Skye put a hand to her heart. "And they rescued their brides from the sea! That's so romantic. Sort of like us."

He cast her a curious glance. "I didn't rescue you from the sea."

"No, but I rescued you in the air."

Another glance. "You crashed me," he reminded.

"The plane tried to crash you," she corrected. "I managed to land you safely."

"In a tree."

She sighed. "You will insist on fussing about that."

He laughed and reached out to pat her knee. "There's no one I'd rather nest with."

HALF AN HOUR LATER Darrick pulled into the driveway that led to the beach house. Skye felt the same instant attachment she'd felt for the house in Edenfield—only this was stronger, deeper.

It was the simple lack of pretension in it, she guessed, perched on a little knoll a small distance from the ocean, with sea grass for a lawn.

It was a wide, two-story structure with a full front porch that wrapped around on the north side. It had gingerbread trim on the center-gabled first and second levels and a carved, open-work railing around the porch that had columns at eight- or ten-foot intervals. It had been painted white with green trim and shutters.

Skye, standing at the foot of the porch steps, ignored the steady drizzle and opened her arms as though to embrace the house. "It's a magical place," she said reverently. "I can feel it. I'll bet one of the Buckleys lived here."

Darrick stood beside her, a carrier in each hand, a blanket over each, protecting the babies from the rain. "Close," he said. "The oldest Buckley brother built it for his firstborn son when he got married. But after that the Buckleys produced a lot of girls who followed husbands around the country, and the house was finally sold out of the family after World War II."

"Isn't that sad?" she said with a gusty sigh.

Darrick led the way up the steps. "Depends on how you choose to look at it. It would be nice if it'd stayed within the family, but life's not a museum, it's an active, kinetic force that moves people around. And I don't think I'd want a child of mine bound forever to a house because I'd passed it on to him. Her," he corrected himself with a grin as he set the carriers down on the porch and dug into a pocket for the front door key.

"Well, that's very noble," Skye said as he fitted the key in the lock. "But women have a different attitude about their homes. I'd want this to be owned by a McKeon until there are Dairy Queens and ATMs on Mars."

He pushed the door open for her but caught her chin in his hand before she could step inside. "But you're standing here with me, a thousand miles from everything you know."

She stood up on tiptoe to kiss him quickly. "Nothing I knew mattered until you," she said matter-of-factly, then walked past him into the house.

It was amazing, Darrick thought, following her inside and closing the door, how she could shake him to the marrow of his bones with a simple string of words. And yet she did it repeatedly, and with seemingly little awareness that she did.

It disturbed him to think about how lonely she must have been as a child, how heartbroken she had to have been when her marriage fell apart. She was so open and so trusting. Life was hard for people with no natural skepticism.

He remembered clearly that he'd developed a healthy dose of it when he was seven and Donovan died. Suddenly life was no longer about the backyard and the park on the corner, about dogs and baseball and bikes. It had become about loss, and that had changed everything.

But it was hard to think about loss now with his hands full of sleeping babies and with Skye wandering through the decrepit house and exclaiming excitedly as though it were a palace.

The deep, wide living room was a dirty shade of lavender accentuated by the gray light coming in through the long windows.

She stopped to admire a small but beautifully carved fireplace now dusty and dingy with neglect. Then she paused on the threshold to the dining room to run a hand along the simple woodwork that arched elegantly in the doorway with decorative canthus leaves at the point where the woodwork bowed.

The kitchen had been remodeled, probably in the sixties, and was a sort of poison yellow in color. An ancient wood cookstove stood in one corner beside its more contemporary cousin and a small but functioning refrigerator. A rickety church pew stood under a window across the room.

Skye spotted the old range and gasped.

"What?" He went toward her in concern, wondering if it harbored a raccoon or a snake.

"Look at it!" she said in a tone that suggested it was something remarkable. She blew dust off the top of it, then coughed.

The stove was a remarkable monstrosity of black enamel, gaudily ornamented with nickel bands, shelves and handles. It had drawers, a fair-size oven, and a deep well for wood.

Skye opened a little door with a twisted handle and

peered inside. "It's wonderful!" She closed the door again and peered into shelves and other cubbyholes. "This was just left with the house? These are usually prized by antiques dealers and collectors."

"Dill and Dunk and I just thought it'd be good to have something to cook on when the wind picks up and the power goes out. Or just for keeping the place warm in winter."

She put her hands on it protectively. "What a prize! Can't you just imagine sitting around it in the winter in this wonderful old place?"

"I wouldn't get too possessive about it," he warned. "Dillon's an excellent cook. Quiche, cioppino, sauces. You name it. He usually eats out of care packages when he's doing relief work, so he loves to cook when he's home. And he thought it was great, too."

"And he'll be coming to the house?"

"Eventually. Come on. I'll show you the rest of the place."

She loved the screened-in sunporch in the back and the extra room on the other side of the kitchen.

"We thought this'd be a good room for the folks when they visit," he said. "They won't have to deal with stairs. And there's a bathroom off the kitchen."

"That's thoughtful," she said with a grin, "but I wouldn't tell them it's because you don't want them to have to climb stairs."

"Duncan said the same thing. He suggested we plant roses outside the window because Mom loves them and tell them that's why they're assigned that room."

"Very diplomatic. All other bedrooms are up-stairs?"

"Right. Lead on."

Darrick followed Skye up. "We've already chosen rooms," he said. "The two in the front are pretty much the same, except for the slope of the eaves on different sides. Those are Dillon's and Duncan's. Both of them have a thing for the ocean. This room's ours."

He walked into a room that stretched across the back of the house with a view of a broad lawn, a thick stand of evergreens and hills rolling inland behind them.

Skye leaned both hands on the dusty windowsill and took in the view. "What a wonderful place for barbecues and croquet and badminton." She sighed and turned to him. "It's like you plucked this place right out of my dreams."

"I told you our relationship was a cosmic decision," he said with a smile, then set the carriers down and looked around the room. "Shall I do our room first?"

She sat on the windowsill and looked around with him. "Maybe your parents' room would be better. With the babies downstairs, I'll be accessible to them and to you. I can help you while they're napping and still hear them easily."

"You don't think the noise will wake them?"

She shrugged. "Sometimes a whisper wakes them, and sometimes they'll sleep through Dori's *Phantom of the Opera* CD played at full volume."

He pulled a face. "*I* could sleep through *Phantom of the Opera* played at full volume."

Skye laughed. "Be nice. Doesn't Dori have a room?"

"She does." He went back into the hallway, reached up to pull a folded stairway down from the ceiling. "She gets the attic where she can work quietly on her precious old authors without disturbance from the rest of us. Go have a look."

Skye climbed the ladder until her upper body disappeared and she could lean her elbows on the attic floor.

Darrick enjoyed the sight of her neat backside and long legs in the khaki shorts Dori had lent her.

"Are there critters up here?" she asked a little nervously, apparently choosing to go no farther.

"Don't think so," he called up to her without taking his eyes off her inspiring form. "We didn't see evidence of anything."

"Good." Her weight shifted to one hip and it was all he could do to restrain himself from putting a hand up to it. A certain careful respect was guiding this relationship and he wanted to honor it. "It's like you've stepped back in time up here with the old dress form and the mirror. Dori should love it. Wrong continent, but right era for her romantic inclinations."

He climbed up beside her and looked into the opening she occupied. "What form? What mirror?"

She looked down at him. "There's an old dress form up here with a beaded bodice on it. And one of those long cheval glass mirrors. Did they just leave it with the house, too?"

"There wasn't anything up there when Dill and Dunk and I looked through the house."

"Well, there is now."

Darrick followed her up as she climbed the rest of the way into the attic. It smelled of antiseptic cleaner, but the slightly sweet, slightly musty smell of old places lingered underneath.

The rafters were bare, and a plank floor had been

laid years ago in the long room with its deeply sloping eaves. There was nothing else in it but the dress form and the mirror—that *hadn't* been there when he and his brothers had toured the house.

Covering the form from neck to waist was what appeared to be the yellowed top of a white dress with a ruffled band collar. Pearl beads were worked through it from the shoulder in a V shape to the point below the waist. The sleeves were also pointed and decorated with bead work.

"The Realtor must have left it," he said, because he didn't know how else to explain it.

"Why?" Skye asked, touching the beadwork.

"I don't know. Maybe it was in a closet or something and we missed it when we looked through the house. She probably took it out when she had the place cleaned for us, then put it back afterward." Yes. That was logical.

Skye turned to smile at him. Her face was a mere inch from his, and he could see a delighted speculation in her eyes. "I think it belonged to one of the dancers and she brought it to us as a welcome gift," she said.

He studied her closely, torn between a need to groan and a need to kiss her until she was senseless.

"One of the dancers."

She smiled dreamily as she turned back to the dress form. "Uh-huh."

"You mean a ghost?"

She turned to him again and looped her arms around his neck. "I mean a friendly spirit who might have been forced to leave this house in body, but whose heart stayed behind."

"But the dancer didn't live here," he pointed out, struggling to maintain reason as the sun peered out

PLAY "LUCKY 7" AND GET
THREE FREE GIFTS!

HOW TO PLAY:

1. With a coin, carefully scratch off the silver box at the right. Then check the claim chart to see what we have for you — **FREE BOOKS** and a gift — **ALL YOURS! ALL FREE!**

2. Send back this card and you'll receive brand-new Harlequin American Romance® novels. These books have a cover price of $3.99 each, but they are yours to keep absolutely free.

3. There's no catch. You're under no obligation to buy anything. We charge nothing —  ZERO — for your first shipment. And you don't have to make any minimum number of purchases — not even one!

4. The fact is thousands of readers enjoy receiving books by mail from the Harlequin Reader Service® months before they're available in stores. They like the convenience of home delivery and they love our discount prices!

5. We hope that after receiving your free books you'll want to remain a subscriber. But the choice is yours — to continue or cancel, any time at all! So why not take us up on our invitation, with no risk of any kind. You'll be glad you did!

YOURS FREE!

PLAY LUCKY 7 FOR THIS EXCITING FREE GIFT!

THIS SURPRISE MYSTERY GIFT COULD BE YOURS FREE WHEN YOU PLAY

LUCKY 7!

NO COST! NO OBLIGATION TO BUY!
NO PURCHASE NECESSARY!

The Harlequin Reader Service® — Here's how it works

Accepting free books places you under no obligation to buy anything. You may keep the books and gift and return the shipping statement marked "cancel." If you do not cancel, about a month later we'll send you 4 additional novels, and bill you just $3.34 each, plus 25¢ delivery per book and applicable sales tax, if any.* That's the complete price — and compared to cover prices of $3.99 each — quite a bargain! You may cancel at any time, but if you choose to continue, every month we'll send you 4 more books, which you may either purchase at the discount price...or return to us and cancel your subscription.

*Terms and prices subject to change without notice. Sales tax applicable in N.Y.

If offer card is missing write to: Harlequin Reader Service, 3010 Walden Ave., P.O. Box 1867, Buffalo, NY 14240-1867

BUSINESS REPLY MAIL
FIRST-CLASS MAIL   PERMIT NO. 717   BUFFALO, NY

POSTAGE WILL BE PAID BY ADDRESSEE

HARLEQUIN READER SERVICE
3010 WALDEN AVE
PO BOX 1867
BUFFALO NY 14240-9952

NO POSTAGE
NECESSARY
IF MAILED
IN THE
UNITED STATES

from behind the clouds and filled the room with a sudden, cozy light. "Her son and daughter-in-law did."

She tried to fix him with a threatening expression that was thwarted by laughter and the affection in her eyes. "Don't mess up my theory with fact."

"Theory," he explained reasonably, "is supposed to be based on fact."

"My intuitive insight, then," she corrected with an insistent grin.

He'd just decided on the kiss over the groan when the first squeal of protest came from one of the babies in the carrier at the foot of the stairs. That meant the next two hours would be occupied with feeding, burping, playing and rocking. There would be no time for kissing.

"There is no friendly spirit," he felt compelled to say as he backed down the ladder, reaching a hand up to guide her down. "The Realtor left the dress form."

"Fine," she said cheerfully, kneeling over the baby carrier. "We'll ask her when we go to town for paint and cleaning supplies."

EVERYONE STOPPED to coo over the twins. Darrick pushed them in the stroller since the sun had made a wide break in the clouds, and Skye walked beside him.

Strangers on the street stopped to peer in at the sleeping babies—women, couples, even a group of teenage girls.

"You must be one of the McKeon boys," one older man said as his wife offered motherly advice to Skye. "I'm Cliff Fisher. This is my wife Roberta."

Darrick shook hands with him, clearly puzzled that

he knew his name. "I am one of the McKeons. Darrick. But how do you...?"

"Our daughter's your Realtor," he said. "I asked about you because Bertie and I live on the next lot. I saw you and two other young men look at the place a couple of months ago, then I didn't see you again. Will you just be summering here?"

Darrick explained about his brothers having work that kept them away much of the time. "But one or the other of us will probably be coming and going all summer long while we fix the place up. My wife and I live just south of Portland, so hopefully we'll be coming down for weekends throughout the year."

"Wonderful. We need a little excitement and some children around here. We're mostly sedate, retired folks."

The brief encounter ended with Bertie promising to stop by with a welcome gift for the babies.

"We should invite them to dinner some time," Skye said to Darrick as they walked on.

"Dinner?" Darrick grinned at her eagerness to extend an invitation. "Have you forgotten the condition of the house and the fact that we have nothing to sit on? And no table?"

She smiled, apparently unaware of any difficulty. "We'll have to find something in a secondhand store to tide us over for the time we're here, anyway. We'll just buy four chairs instead of two. I don't think the Fishers will care that it isn't Chippendale. And we'll have *company*. Nobody ever visited us when I was a child. I want to have lots of company."

He found himself more and more anxious to give her what she wanted—whatever it was. "When my family starts filling the house, there won't be room left for company, but we'll do our best. Did Bertie tell you that the Realtor who sold us the house is her daughter?''

"Yes, she did. Polly somebody."

"Warriner. And I'll bet you asked her about the dress form and the mirror."

Skye looked both defensive and sheepish. "Yes, I did."

"And?"

"And she didn't know if her daughter had returned anything to the house or not. So we'll just have to ask her directly."

"*You* have to ask her," he said, denying complicity. "I'm happy believing she found the stuff in a closet and returned it after she had the house cleaned for us."

Skye shook her head at him pityingly. "Fine. Then you can wait outside of the office with the girls. Where is it, anyway?"

Darrick turned the stroller down a sidestreet of the atmospheric little waterfront town. Old board-and-batten architecture was interspersed with postwar storefronts, but everything downtown was freshly painted and streetlights were hung with colorful baskets of flowers.

Every block had a wooden bench under a flowering crab apple tree. Right in the middle of town was a five-story hotel complete with shutters and a second-level veranda. It was painted gray with white trim, and tall white letters identified it as the Buckley Arms.

"So one of the brothers and his dancer went into the hotel business," Skye observed. "I feel as though I'm getting to know them."

He pulled her back onto the curb as she stepped into the street, her eyes still on the hotel. "Just so long as you don't *join* them. Watch where you're going. The light's red."

They crossed when the light turned green, and Darrick led her halfway down the block to a narrow store-front whose window was filled with photographs of houses for sale.

"When she questions your sanity and asks you to leave," Darrick said seriously, "we'll be waiting right here."

She gave him a scornful arch of her eyebrow and went into the office.

She was out in a few minutes with the attractive woman who'd worked very hard to get Darrick and his brothers the best deal with the best terms.

Polly extended her hand to Darrick with a welcoming smile. "Hi!" she said effusively. "How nice to see you back. Everyone around here will be delighted to see a family in that house. I understand you've met my parents."

"Yes." He mentioned that her mother said she'd be coming to visit.

She laughed. "They love to talk. My mother knows all the gossip, and my father keeps up on the news, so be prepared to learn everyone's life history, and to have an opinion on current events." Her eyes stopped on the stroller, then she leaned into it, hands clasped at her breast. "Are these *yours?*"

"Yes." Skye pointed to the sleeping baby in the pink bonnet and blanket. "That's Michelle." Then the one in mint green. "And Gabrielle."

The woman whispered endearments over them, then straightened to look at Darrick in puzzlement. "I got the impression you and your brothers were all single."

The explanation was too complicated. "That's

changed," Darrick said simply. "Skye and I got married last week and we're going to try to get a couple of rooms painted, and maybe some work done on the roof while we're here."

She nodded, clearly puzzled but discreet enough to ask no questions.

"Polly knows nothing about the dress form and the mirror," Skye said with an air of innocence belied by the "gotcha!" look in her eye. "She has no idea who put them there."

Darrick didn't want to encourage Skye's belief that the presence of those things was somehow supernatural, but he didn't know how to explain it, either. Though he felt sure there had to be a logical answer.

"The Heritage House ladies had been hoping to get your property last year to set up a Dancer's Beach museum," Polly said. "But they couldn't get the funding and finally withdrew their bid. A few of them are a little eccentric, but I can't imagine them breaking into the house to put a couple of the artifacts in your attic."

"I think they were a gift from one of the dancers," Skye said.

Darrick drew a breath, bracing himself to defend her from Polly's scornful laughter. But Polly seemed to consider that possibility instead.

"Olivia was supposed to have had a couple of psychic episodes," she said. "You'll have to ask my mother about it. She's put together a history of the Buckleys that she's self-published."

The telephone rang in the office, and Polly excused herself to answer it, shouting a goodbye as she hurried inside.

"Ha!" Skye said to Darrick, straining up on tiptoe

to deliver the "told-you-so" nose to nose. "Olivia left them!"

"Olivia," he said, leaning over her as she settled back on her heels, "has gone to her reward, and I doubt seriously that she's spending eternity buying antiques for you!" He'd lowered his voice and added the last on an emphatic whisper. "Now could we concentrate on why we came to town? You're going to help me pick out paint, remember?"

"The trouble with you," she said, pushing the stroller toward the main street, "is that you haven't spent enough time in the sky."

"Last time I tried to spend time in the sky," he returned with a smile and a thank-you to a passerby who admired the twins, "someone crashed me into a tree."

She stopped in the middle of the sidewalk to frown at him impatiently. "Are you still going to be bringing that up when we're in our walkers? I meant that when you're up in the clouds, reality has different boundaries. Life and death, fantasy and reality, sort of pass each other. There's a place where they're side by side and what you once considered outrageous…doesn't seem so impossible anymore."

"Skye," he said, using a gentle tone despite his exasperation, "I know what you're saying, but that isn't true for me. I work in a hospital. For me there's an absolute difference between life and death. And I've never had trouble distinguishing fantasy from reality. If you want to believe Olivia put the dress form and the mirror in the attic, go ahead. But don't try to convert me, okay?"

"Okay," she said in the same gentle tone, "but how do you explain it?"

"I don't have to explain it. I'm content to just let it be."

"Without an answer? Doesn't that upset your ever-so-practical persona?"

"No, because I'm sure there's an answer out there. I just don't know what it is."

"Really." She tossed her hair and pushed the stroller forward. "Well, I do."

They bought six gallons of a toxin-free soft white paint and a cordless roller, three gallons of a bright white semi-gloss for the woodwork, and several brushes.

"You think that'll be enough for the whole downstairs?" Skye asked. They sat on a tarpaulin on the floor, leaning against the wall, each feeding a baby, and stared at the collection of paint and tools grouped in the middle of the otherwise empty living room.

"I don't know," Darrick answered. "It's supposed to be high-hiding stuff, but I don't know how efficient the pump-pack roller will be as opposed to brushes."

She shook her head. "Imagine a tube that connects the roller to a container of paint you wear over your shoulder with a strap. The Buckleys would be amazed."

"Mmm." Darrick had leaned his head back against the wall and closed his eyes, Gabrielle staring blankly from the crook of his arm, finally bored with her formula.

Michelle still drank greedily.

"What do you want for dinner?" Skye asked, absorbing the peace of the moment.

"Why don't you wait and see if Olivia drops anything off," Darrick teased lazily, and he put the bottle down and shifted Gabrielle to his shoulder.

Skye didn't want to laugh, but she couldn't help herself. She would have elbowed him, but for the baby in his arms.

"We brought cereal with us," she said. "Soup and crackers, and a few other canned goods."

"We have no pots and pans," he reminded her.

She gave him a superior glance. "Yes, we do. I packed a small frying pan and a saucepan in the picnic basket. Along with dishes and table service for four."

He opened his eyes and rolled his head toward her, still patting the baby. "You're pretty domestic for a flyer."

"I just didn't want to risk going hungry."

"Soup sounds great," he said. "Whoever's baby goes to sleep first has to fix it."

"Deal."

"WELL, I'D LIKE A REMATCH." Skye pretended displeasure as she stirred soup in a pan while Darrick paced behind her with a whiny Gabrielle. "It doesn't seem fair that because I'm more skilled and efficient at getting a baby to sleep that I also have to fix dinner."

Darrick grinned. "Stop whining. You agreed to the deal."

"But Gabrielle finished eating first. I thought that meant you'd end up doing it."

"Cheaters never prosper."

"It wasn't cheating," she denied as she rummaged in the picnic basket for a pair of mugs. "It was…the creative use of facts in hand."

"Skye McKeon," he said, stopping to rock Gabrielle back and forth as she finally stopped fussing and began to close her eyes, "you have one clever line of bull after the other. How do you come up with them?''

Skye felt her entire body flush with reaction. She kept her face averted while she stirred soup. ''Just…gifted, I guess.''

She felt a nibble on the back of her neck followed by a kiss. Then Darrick leaned a hip against the counter so that he could look into her face.

''Why are you blushing?'' he asked lightly. ''Are you embarrassed that you have a clever line of bull?''

She concentrated on the pan. ''Of course not. And it's not a blush, it's the heat from the soup.''

''Morc bull. I think you were blushing because you were fantasizing about me.''

She bit back a grin and glanced at him as she poured soup into the pair of mugs. ''You think so?''

He nodded, lowering his voice now that Gabrielle was asleep. His eyes were filled with humor but also with clear sexual suggestion. ''I do. I think when you told me you were gifted, you were thinking about other ways you'd be able to prove that to me in the future.''

She rolled her eyes. ''The distant future.''

He frowned. ''Don't remind me. I'm going to put Gabrielle down. Be right back.''

The soup poured, Skye took a moment to draw a deep, steadying breath while he was out of the room.

''Keep it together, girl,'' she told herself in a firm whisper. ''Keep it together.''

DARRICK HAD already given the living room and dining room one coat of paint and was at work on the second the following afternoon when the mailman arrived with a package.

Skye, atop the ladder and painting the window frame on the first finished wall, rested her brush across the can of paint and climbed down to investigate.

As the mailman handed the package to Darrick, a loud chiming sound came from within the box. The mailman grinned. "That's proof that it arrived in working order."

Skye closed the door as Darrick carried the box to the middle of the living room floor. "I *love* a chiming clock," she said, kneeling beside him as he slit the tape that held the box closed.

"The first thing we're going to do," Darrick said, folding the sides of the box down and pulling out wads of protective paper, "is disconnect the chiming mechanism."

"Why?" she asked.

"Because we'll have babies up every half hour instead of every two hours." That explanation made, he sat back on his heels, a puff of wadded paper in his hands, and stared into the box. "Geez," he said with a wince. "How do they always manage to top themselves?"

Skye patted the paper out of her way so that she could see what had put the horrified expression on Darrick's face.

She too stared in disbelief for a moment, then put a hand to her mouth to stifle laughter.

The box contained an old-fashioned and apparently very genuine horse collar. It was fairly large, covered in leather, and some creative person had fitted an old clock with classic Roman numerals into the opening.

It was the ugliest thing Skye had ever seen, and she fell in love with it instantly. She reached into the box to take it out and found she couldn't lift it.

Darrick pulled her hands away from it. "It's going to take a couple of molly screws to hold this weight. Who do you suppose would put a clock in a horse collar?"

"Someone who rode his horse to appointments and was always late?" Skye suggested helpfully.

He groaned. "This collar would be for pulling a wagon or a plow."

She didn't see the problem. "Well, those things would have to be done in a timely fashion. I love it. I think we should hang it over the fireplace as soon as that wall's finished."

Darrick shook his head and began to repack the box. "No. Dillon and Duncan and I made a deal. I paint, Dillon brings in furniture, and Duncan does the garden and buys the barbecue and lawn furniture. We all pitch in to pay for everything, but the responsibilities have been assigned. The horse-collar clock is Dill's problem."

"But your parents are coming for Memorial Day. What if Dillon isn't home yet?" She rose up on her knees, hands on her hips. "They'll want to see it hanging somewhere."

He opened his mouth to offer a solution, but she interrupted quickly with, "And not in a closet or in the attic."

He accepted defeat. "You win. I'll hang it over the fireplace. But you're the one who has to take the flack when my brothers harrass me about it."

"Oh, come on." She swatted his shoulder and stood. "It's from your parents. It doesn't matter what it looks like. It represents love, just like the settee. It'll be beautiful."

Darrick thought beautiful might be too strong a

word, but as he stood with Skye in front of the fireplace the following afternoon to admire the now-hanging horse-collar clock, he thought it had a certain...funky appeal.

"Maybe I should tuck a few flowers in it," Skye suggested. Gabrielle sat in her arms and studied the scene with a wide-eyed wonder that moved her tiny mouth into mysterious shapes. "What do you think Gabby?"

Darrick held Michelle on his arm in the football carry. She gurgled and grunted, apparently content.

"Then it'll look like some poor horse was forced to run the Kentucky Derby in that collar," he objected.

Skye giggled. "But it'll look like he won."

An emphatic knock sounded on the door. He and Skye looked at each other in puzzlement.

"It's either someone representing a door-to-door religion," he said as he went to the door, Skye trailing him, "or you have an Avon lady."

He was wrong. Skye stared in disbelief and abject terror at their visitor. It was Tommy Fennerty.

Chapter Nine

Skye looked into her ex-husband's handsome face and was momentarily paralyzed and speechless. Tommy Fennerty had poisoned the memories of the only two happy years in her past, and now had the potential to disintegrate her future.

As she stared at him, she saw his eyes go over her with all the old familiar merriment and affection she'd once so loved about him. Then his eyes went to the baby in her arms and the merriment was replaced by confusion.

His gaze moved with increased puzzlement to Darrick, standing beside her, and the baby in his arms. Then his eyes swung back to hers. She could have sworn she heard a clang.

Her brain awoke with a sudden, wily reaction to danger.

"Tommy!" she said, forcing a tone of pleased surprise. She caught his arm in her free hand and pulled him into the living room. She was aware of Darrick stepping aside to give him space.

She turned to Darrick as they all stood in a tight knot just inside the door. "Darrick, this is my ex-husband, Tommy Fennerty. Tommy, this is my…my present husband, Darrick McKeon.''

Her heart beat so wildly it threatened to choke her as she watched the men shake hands.

Tommy was as tall as Darrick, but more thickly built. He had a lighthearted, happy-go-lucky air that had once so appealed to her and now seemed ineffectual beside Darrick's easy competence and self-assurance.

''And…the babies?'' Tommy asked with a glance from one to the other. ''Ours,'' Darrick replied—a little testily, Skye thought. ''I have Michelle, and Skye's holding Gabrielle.''

''Well, I'll be damned.'' Tommy leaned over the twin in Darrick's arms with genuine delight. ''Aren't you the prettiest little thing. The world's full of miracles, isn't it?''

''What are you doing here, Tommy?'' Skye asked quickly. ''I thought you were running a flight school in Kansas somewhere.''

''I was.'' He straightened and rubbed an index finger gently over the head of the baby she held. ''But I'm selling the Seneca and going to work for a commercial airline.''

''You're kidding!'' For an instant Skye forgot the threat he posed in her astonishment over that bit of information. Tommy was Waldo Pepper come to life.

''But you always said you'd go down with the Seneca before you'd work for someone else.''

He shrugged in self-deprecation. ''Big talk. Now suddenly I need regular hours and health insurance.''

Skye was able to guess why even before he added almost apologetically, ''I'm getting married.''

She was shocked when the old pain rose up to smite

her. She didn't love him anymore, though she would always treasure memories of their friendship. But she hadn't thought she'd ever recover from the way he'd made her feel. Until Darrick.

"Tommy, that's wonderful," she said, but her voice came out thin and small and though her eyes were averted from Darrick, she saw his quick look at her. "Anyone I know?"

Tommy shook his head. "No. She signed up for flying lesson and turns out she's a major Yankees fan, too."

Skye caught her breath and managed to make her voice sound more normal. "Well, that sounds like a marriage made in heaven. So...how did you find me? And why?"

Darrick slid his free arm under Gabrielle to take the baby from her. "Why don't you take Tommy into the kitchen," he suggested politely, "where there's at least a place to sit down, and I'll keep these two entertained. I think there's coffee in the pot."

"Okay. Thanks." As Darrick went into the bedroom with the twins, Skye led Tommy into the kitchen and pointed him to the pew. "I'm afraid that's all we have in the way of furniture at the moment." While she poured coffee and instinctively added the two sugars Tommy put in it, she carried on chattily about the state of the house—how Darrick and his brothers had bought it and had each undertaken a part of the redecorating.

Tommy, always restless, opened the back door and looked out. "Can we have our coffee on the back porch steps?"

"Sure." Cups in hand she stepped through the door he held open, pausing just long enough to hand him his. She noticed in dismay that her hands were shaking.

The afternoon was cloudy and cool, but she was comfortable—physically, at least—in a pair of old coveralls from her Mariposa days. She sat on the top step, and Tommy sat a step below her, turning to look up at her.

"You left your phone number in Edenfield with Marty Clements at Mariposa," he said, "so I called there and reached a young woman who seemed to be in a flap about something. She said she was your sister-in-law, and that you were here."

So Dori was home. But in a flap? A corner of her mind wondered what Dori had been upset about, but Tommy had leaned an elbow on the stair on which Skye sat and leaned closer. She braced herself for the question she'd been expecting him to ask from the moment she'd opened the door and found him standing there.

"You adopted twins?" he asked quietly.

She wished she could simply say yes, but she still didn't know why he was here. And if Darrick decided to join them for coffee and Tommy mentioned the adoption…

"No," she replied, warming her hands on her cup. "They're Darrick's."

"Wife died?"

"No."

"Left him?"

"No." She gave him a look that told him he owed her. "He thinks they're ours from a night last September when I was flying him to San Diego and we went down in the Siskiyous. And I'd consider it a personal favor if you refrain from setting him straight."

She saw all the questions that came to mind move across his gaze.

"You don't have to understand it," she said sharply. "You just have to cooperate. I presume after our experience, you've had the soon-to-be second Mrs. Fennerty tested for fertility?"

It was a nasty question and she'd promised herself the day he walked out that she'd never be nasty about it, but she thought perhaps the uniqueness of the moment allowed her that frailty.

But he didn't seem hurt, just regretful. "I'm sorry, Skye," he said. "I tried to explain."

He had. He'd been as tearful as she had been over the news that the ruptured appendix she'd had after they were married had resulted in peritonitis that had necessitated the removal of both ovaries. Only she'd had to live with the diagnosis of infertility while he'd opted not to.

"I know it wasn't fair to you, but you know how I love kids."

"I do," she said. Then added to herself *more than you loved me*.

She took a deep sip of the coffee and couldn't decide which tasted more bitter——it or her memories. She put both aside.

"Why'd you come, Tommy?"

He pulled a folded document out of his pocket. "We were a little casual about things in the divorce settlement and I need you to sign off on the Seneca so I can sell it."

"Of course." By mutual agreement, they'd divided their little two-plane fleet. She took the document from him and he handed her a pen. She signed where he indicated and handed both back to him.

"Skye." Tommy pocketed the document and pen, then fixed her with a concerned expression that reminded her of the friendship they'd once shared. "I know I'm not the one who should be second-guessing anyone's behavior, and I can't begin to imagine how this happened, but do you think it's smart? I mean, letting McKeon think you're the mother of the babies? What if she comes back?"

"She abandoned them in the hospital."

"Well…what if it comes up? Over a lifetime together, there's bound to be a time when he'll have access to your health records or something will…"

"I'll deal with it then," she said, getting to her feet. "You want to stay for dinner?"

He stood also and studied her for a moment as though he had something more to say. Then he apparently decided it was none of his business. She wasn't surprised. He'd dismissed her problems very easily once before.

"No, thanks," he said. "I flew over and promised I'd be back as soon as possible."

"All right. Are you at Foxglove Field?"

"Yes. I took a cab in."

"Come on. I'll drive you back."

DARRICK CAUGHT HIMSELF pacing. He told himself that it was all right. He was pacing because there was nowhere to sit. It didn't mean that he was jealous of Skye's ex-husband, or that he was suspicious because she said she'd be back in half an hour and that that had been almost three hours ago.

He leaned a shoulder against a window frame still a little tacky from its second coat of paint and frowned at the cloudy sky. He'd thought marriage would feel more secure than this. He'd thought such a bold step would mean that both parties were sure of what they wanted.

Of course theirs had begun in a completely unconventional way, so it wasn't reasonable to expect the old standards to apply. And she'd been married once before. He'd seen men and women embittered and angry over whatever had ended their relationship, but Skye and Fennerty seemed more saddened by whatever had ended theirs.

And he could remember clearly the sound of Skye's voice that moment in the upside-down plane when she'd come to consciousness and she'd thought he was Tommy. It had been hopeful, eager.

And today, though they'd been simply polite to each other, he'd seen the regret in Fennerty's eyes—and the curious fear in Skye's. The fear of losing Tommy irretrievably? he wondered.

He saw the Lexus speed into view and turn into the driveway with a precision that had to have been luck rather than skill at that speed. There was a squeal of brakes, and he drew in a breath as the car finally rocked to a stop less than an inch from the garage doors.

He tore the front door open and ran out to her, expecting that display of offensive driving to mean she'd been sobbing as she drove home, upset about Tommy's marriage.

But she was all smiles when she stepped out of the car. "Hi!" she said cheerfully. She put her hands on his shoulders and gave him a quick kiss. "Sorry I'm late, but you won't believe what I found!"

He followed her to the trunk of the car. "Are you

all right?'' he asked. ''The way you barreled into the driveway I thought…''

She grinned at him as she beeped the trunk open. ''I always drive that way. I'm a pilot.''

He wasn't sure whether to be relieved that she didn't seem traumatized by Tommy's visit, or concerned about the future safety of the driving public.

The open trunk revealed two wooden chairs, one white and ladderbacked, the other a captain's chair in unfinished oak with a gouge in the seat. ''Would you believe I got these for five bucks apiece? We can just put a cushion over the gouge on that one. And look at these.''

She caught his wrist and drew him around the car to the passenger seat where another chair had been overturned on the seat and belted in. She unfastened the belt and handed the simple Shaker chair out to him.

''They're a little banged up,'' she said, opening the back door. ''But they're not rickety.'' She handed out another chair that matched the Shaker, then reached in to pull out an old gateleg table that had been folded to fit in the car. ''Isn't this perfect? A little paint and these'll be perfectly serviceable in the kitchen until Dillon gets around to buying furniture. Of course we won't have time for that tonight.''

A chair in each hand, he started for the back door into the kitchen. She tried to follow with the table, then deciding it was too heavy, leaned it against the car and picked up the other two chairs instead.

''Time for what?'' he asked when she caught up with him.

''For painting.'' She sounded breathless so he

slowed his pace. "We'll have to just wash them down."

"We can do that tomorrow. You sound worn out." He put the chairs down, opened the door for her, then picked them up again and followed her in.

"I invited the Fishers for dinner," she said with a smile he was just beginning to decide was a little too wide and matched a manner a little too forcedly cheerful.

She headed out again, avoiding his eyes, and pulled two grocery bags out of the back of the car. "I just suggested spaghetti and salad and they thought that was fine." She delved into the bag and handed him a box of Raisinettes. "You don't mind that I invited them, do you? I just ran into them in the grocery store, and Bertie said she'd made some things for the twins, and it just seemed like a neighborly thing to do. If you'll get one of these bags, I'll come back out and help you with the table, then if you can scrub it all down while I'm cooking…"

And she talked nonstop until the Fishers arrived an hour and a half later.

He let her have at it, thinking any effort on his part to try to stop her and make her explain what this clearly emotional and panicky spate of good cheer was all about would only further upset her. And if she told him it meant she'd decided she loved Tommy Fennerty after all and didn't think she could stay with him, he wasn't sure what he would do.

The babies were up when the Fishers arrived, and each insisted on commandeering one while Skye served wine. She'd bought a lounge cushion for the pew, and Darrick was surprised by how much more comfortable that made it.

"We have five grandchildren," Bertie said wistfully, "but they're all far away, and we never get to see them except occasionally at Christmas."

She handed a white box toward Darrick while Skye gave the sauce a stir, then came to the pew to investigate.

Darrick opened it, and in a nest of tissue found two little brimmed cotton hats in a baby animal print in bright, primary colors. He held one up in each hand for Skye to see.

She came to stand at his shoulder and take one of the hats for a closer inspection. Her face was wreathed in smiles, and he took comfort in the fact that whatever she felt about him, she was truly enjoying her motherhood.

He wondered idly what path her life would have taken if she hadn't gotten pregnant that night on the mountain. Or how his life would have been different.

Whatever might have been, he thought, could never have measured up to this. He couldn't bear the thought of losing it now.

Bertie brought his attention back to the box with a pointing finger. "There's more in the next layer of tissue."

He delved into it and pulled out two of something made in the same fabric—but he couldn't identify what they were. They had straps and a padded buckle adjustment, but the construction didn't quite make sense to him.

"Front packs?" Skye guessed.

Bertie confirmed that with a nod. "I've made them for all my grandchildren. Babies love to be carried so they can look at you." She put Michelle in Cliff's free arm, then stood to fit the contraption onto Skye. Then she reclaimed the baby and put her into the middle of the fabric.

And suddenly it all made sense. Tiny legs protruded out the sides, and Michelle stared up at Skye with that perpetually amazed expression.

The women laughed, then Bertie took the other one and tried it on Darrick. He sat docilely while she worked over him.

"I made longer straps on this one," she said as she adjusted the pack on him. "To accommodate those shoulders." She slipped the left strap on, then she eased Gabrielle into it.

The twin looked at him for one startled moment, then leaned her head against him and went to sleep.

"Looks like a perfect fit to me," Cliff said. Then he sniffed the air appreciatively. "Smells wonderful. Homemade sauce?"

Skye, still sporting the baby, went back to the stove. "No. Just a little garlic and basil added to bottled sauce."

She pointed to the table Darrick had scrubbed down and covered with a simple red and white checkered tablecloth she'd also bought. "Make yourselves comfortable. The pasta will be ready in about a minute."

His wife, Darrick was discovering was a charming hostess, and tonight particularly, she seemed to be driven to tell stories, to listen to Cliff's with rapt attention and ask questions.

Darrick understood that it was all because she didn't want to talk to him—at least not about anything serious. Like Tommy. And what had inspired this hectic mood.

But they were going to settle that when the Fishers went home.

SKYE COULDN'T TELL if it was her guilty conscience at work or simply her imagination, but every time she turned in Darrick's direction she found him watching her. It probably looked like husbandly attention to the Fishers, but she knew him well enough now to know that nothing, however small or thinly defined, escaped his attention.

He couldn't know that she'd waved Tommy off and headed back to Dancer's Beach torn between the need to tell him the truth and stark terror at the prospect of losing him and the twins.

But he was clearly seeing through her transparent subterfuge and wondering why she'd come home a brainless chatterbox with a million things to do to keep them busy—and in the company of other people.

Sooner or later it was going to occur to him that she simply needed time to think. And that would lead him to wonder why. And then he would begin to ask questions.

She desperately needed something else to think about.

"There's a dress form with a half-sewn bodice with pearl beads on it," she told Bertie. "And a full-length mirror. Your daughter thought you might know something about it because of your work with the Heritage House ladies."

Bertie thought a moment, then shook her head. "The County Historical Society Museum in Lincoln City has some of the Buckleys' things, and Minnie Dawson has some things in a climate-controlled room in her basement. Her grandmother was Joshua and Sarajane Buckley's daughter. Joshua was the second Buckley brother. Then there was Mathew. I don't recall Minnie or the museum having a pearled bodice."

"It looks as though someone was making a wedding dress." Skye sipped at her coffee, disappointed that Bertie knew nothing about the beautiful bodice.

"Then it can't have been Olivia's," Bertie said, dipping up a spoon of vanilla ice cream over which Skye had poured crème de menthe for dessert. "She never married. She was a good ten years older than the rest of them, you know. She was in love with Barton, the oldest Buckley brother. Everyone thought they were in love, but he married one of the other dancers instead."

"Do you know why?"

"Barton wanted a big family like the one he'd grown up in. But Olivia had been ill for a while after her rescue from the shipwreck, and the doctor had warned her that her delicate constitution wouldn't favor childbirth. So Barton married the youngest of the dancers—a robust little thing named India."

Skye felt as though someone had struck her on the head with a mallet. Poor Olivia! If anyone could relate to her situation, Skye could. Almost one hundred years separated them, but time was bridged by empathy.

"Would you like to see it?" Skye asked Bertie.

Bertie was out of her chair in an instant.

"Skye." Darrick caught her arm as she, too, stood. "I'm not sure that ladder is a good idea for Bertie."

"We'll only go high enough for her to see through the opening. And I'll stay behind her."

Cliff held his hands out toward her. "Well, at least leave me the baby. And maybe the coffeepot."

"Better bring the step stool," Darrick suggested. "Or you won't be able to reach to pull down the stairs."

"Right." Skye went into the little pantry off the

kitchen for the stool and waved Bertie to follow her. In the hallway upstairs, she placed the stool under the opening and stepped up to pull down the steps.

Bertie moved the stool aside when Skye climbed down and unfolded the stairway. Then she urged Bertie up and followed behind her.

Bertie climbed until her upper body was in the attic. Skye stopped when she was eye level with the floor and heard Bertie's little gasp of surprise.

"My...goodness," she said under her voice, as though the sight called for a reverent quiet. "Look at the size of that waist."

"I know." Skye gripped the floorboards with her hands. "You should see the beadwork up close. It's so perfect. She had to have worked for weeks on it."

"Why do you think it's Olivia's?" Bertie asked.

"I had no idea whose it was at first. But Darrick insists the form and the mirror weren't here when he and his brothers looked at the house. Then when we moved in, here it was—and when I asked your daughter if she'd moved the things out when they asked her to have the house cleaned, then brought them back, she said she hadn't. Then we got to talking about the dancers, and she said Olivia was known to have had some sort of psychic episodes. That she hadn't wanted to come on the boat and then there was the accident."

Bertie turned slightly to look at her. "You mean you think..." She turned back to the form. "That...Olivia...left it?"

Skye sighed. "I'm not sure I really believe that, but I like to think it. It all fits."

"Well, dear, I don't think it does. I mean, Olivia didn't live here. This was one of Barton Buckley's sons' home, built long after Olivia moved away."

"Where did she go?"

"I believe she went on to the Klondike."

"With such delicate health?"

"Well, she might not have survived too long. That's all the family history says about her. But, my point is that this would have been a strange place for her to leave the bodice of her wedding dress, because she stayed at the old Buckley house—which is long gone—until she moved away." Bertie patted Skye's head in an affectionate gesture. "And if this were the work of her...spirit, it seems to me she'd have left it at the museum with the other Buckley things."

"But she never became a Buckley," Skye protested.

"Then it doesn't make sense that she'd leave it here, either. This was a Buckley house—and it wasn't even built until twenty-some years after she left. And the Buckleys who lived here had two sons, so it couldn't belong to them."

"Well..." Skye studied the bodice with a love and warmth she couldn't explain. "Whoever it belonged to, I'm glad it's here. Maybe it doesn't matter why it is."

She backed down the steps and helped Bertie climb down. She listened absently while making another pot of coffee as Bertie told Cliff about the bodice, and the two of them and Darrick tried to analyze who it might belong to and how it had gotten there.

But she thought she knew.

Scientifically she couldn't explain it, but in her heart she was sure that somehow the heavens had opened up and allowed Olivia to leave her this gift. Olivia, who'd been passed over by the man she loved, for a younger, stronger woman who could give him the children he wanted—offered it to Skye, who'd shared a similar fate.

Olivia was lending her support, Skye was sure. She'd given her the single thing she'd possessed that embodied all her hopes and dreams for the future.

Skye smiled at the thought that Olivia was reaching across time to help her.

DARRICK SAW his determination to settle things with Skye tonight disintegrated when Dori arrived in a cab just as the Fishers walked back to their place.

She was loaded down with suitcase, sleeping bag, books, laptop, briefcase, and a purse big enough to require an operator's license.

He and Skye helped her carry it all in, cleared away the dinner dishes while Dori looked in on the twins, then gave her a tour of the house.

"Dill and Dunk and I thought you'd like the attic," Darrick said, standing behind her on the ladder as she looked into the room. "But Skye's convinced the dress form and the mirror are a gift from the great beyond."

"Beyond?" Dori asked, finishing the climb and clamboring up into the space. "You mean as in…death?"

Darrick followed her up, Skye right behind him. Skye launched into an explanation of what she thought and what she'd discovered so far, and Dori listened as she walked around the bodice, touching it lovingly.

Darrick accepted that all hope for a reasonable explanation for the presence of those things was lost. Dori was clearly willing to become a believer.

"Okay, I'm out of here," Darrick said, giving Dori a quick hug. "I don't think you should sleep up here, though, until we get it fixed up for you. And it's a long way down to the first floor that we're using until the second floor's done. If you had a problem, we wouldn't even hear you."

Dori did another turn around the dress form. "You mean if Olivia came to visit me?" she teased.

He groaned. "I mean if you fell or had a nightmare or any other problem of *this* world."

"Ah," she said. "Okay. Maybe I will set up my sleeping bag in one of the second floor bedrooms. It's closer to the fridge, anyway."

"Good. See you in the morning." Darrick started down the stairs but she called his name before he disappeared from view.

She looked suddenly a little embarrassed or uncomfortable. "I...ah...I know I just got back on the job, but if it's okay, I might have to leave again in a couple of days. Just for a day," she added hastily. "One of my professors is coming to the States for the first time, and he said if I could meet him in Seattle, he'd look over my preliminary notes and make sure I'm on the right track."

He suspected she was fibbing. She'd been his little sister long enough for him to recognize the signs— direct eye contact but stark pallor and fidgety fingers.

"Why can't he come here?"

"Well...he doesn't have a car."

"Neither do you."

"But you do."

"You want me to drive you to Seattle?"

"No." She forced a smile. "I want you to lend me the Lexus."

He leaned his forearms on the attic floor and fixed her with a scolding look. "Dori. Honey. You took your driver's test four times before you barely squeaked by with a passing grade."

"Darrick!" Skye frowned at him, then turned to Dori. "Don't worry. I'll fly you there."

"Whoa!" Darrick protested. The only thing he could think of that would worry him more than his little sister driving alone to Seattle was his wife flying her there.

Skye ignored him. "When do you have to be there?"

Dori didn't seem thrilled with the offer. "Well, I'm not sure. It depends on when he arrives. It'll be kind of a last-minute thing. I don't think…"

"Then flying is definitely the way to go," Skye said. Then she returned her attention to the dress. "Can you pinpoint a year for this dress?" she asked Dori. "According to what I've discovered, she…"

Darrick continued down the stairs, then down into the kitchen where he loaded the dishwasher, tidied the kitchen, then carried Dori's bags up to Dillon's room on the left side of the front of the house. He heard laughter and conversation from the attic.

The horse-collar clock read 10:50 when he turned off the bathroom light and climbed into the sleeping bag.

He pretended to be asleep when Skye came to bed half an hour later. He was sure she was tired, after the eventful day and with the twins asleep only feet away, it was no time for confrontation.

But it would have to come eventually. He wondered if she'd avoided conversation all evening because she was reluctant to tell him that she and Tommy had decided they were in love after all. He had said he was getting married, but might have changed his mind if she'd made it clear she still loved him.

Just as the darkness and the quiet made that nightmare seem very plausible, she snuggled into his back, flung her arm around his middle and sighed contentedly.

In a moment she was fast asleep.

And he was wide awake.

Chapter Ten

Darrick concluded that the physical activity of cleaning, sanding and painting was doing a lot for the beach house, but it wasn't doing much for its intended purpose—the alleviation of sexual frustration. It also wasn't helping him deal with Skye's curious behavior and his own jealousy.

Activity helped somewhat during the day, but at night he seemed to be beyond comfort.

When he finished the day exhausted, the state he hoped for, Skye spent all evening pampering him. If he complained of muscle pain, she massaged him with liniment, usually humming while she worked.

He was aware of her every fingertip in contact with the tight muscles at the back of his neck, across his shoulders, down his back.

If he yawned, she settled him on the old flowered sofa they'd bought two days ago at a church rummage sale, propped a pillow under his head, covered him with a light blanket and put on the television for him.

She brought him coffee and snacks and insisted that she and Dori would deal with the twins. And when they were finally down, she came and sat with him, replacing the pillow with her lap and spending hours stroking his hair.

But then every once in a while, when she held one of the twins, or when she stood atop the ladder painting, he would see that frightened look on her face. And if he happened to catch her eye in one of those moments, the fear would change to misery and she would look away.

He was in imminent danger of death from the agonies of wanting her—and of having to know what she was thinking!

On the one hand, she'd given him so much and he wanted to return her generosity.

At this point in her life of love deprivation, he wanted her to know what it was like to receive love as well as give it. He wanted her to know what was in his heart, and words simply couldn't say it.

On the other hand, those looks made him wonder if expressions of love from him would be welcome.

He'd chosen to bide his time, to let her choose the right moment to speak to him about what had changed between them since Tommy's visit. But she didn't seem willing to do that.

So he was going to have to.

During the night he would get up to be with the babies before she could hear them, so that he wouldn't have to look at her, all rumpled and sleepy-eyed in her simple oversize T-shirt, contented and serene, when he was all raging emotions and longings that were close to choking him.

He even agreed to stay home alone with the babies, one day, while she drove Dori to the library for a couple of hours' research. Skye had been talking about looking for more information on the Buckley family and the dancers from San Francisco—Olivia in particular.

He couldn't explain the curious dress form with the silky white dress top on it, but he also couldn't believe that some shipwrecked dancer from one hundred years ago had defied the boundaries of death and brought it to them as a welcome gift.

Of course, Skye knew no such boundaries. She claimed that flight blurred limitations and extended the reach of the mysterious and the unexplainable.

She'd developed some attachment to Olivia she said he simply wouldn't understand.

As though sensing his frustration and desperate need for a few hours of solitude and peace, the angel babies decided to be anything but angels. Gabrielle woke screaming the moment Skye walked out the door. Michelle was awakened by the din before Darrick could even reach the bassinet, and then both babies were in competition to see who could be fussier, angrier, louder.

Darrick alternately rocked and paced with one or the other or both, but nothing worked. Once changed they continued to fuss and refused bottle or pacifier.

In a moment of dark amusement, he related to their frustration. They wanted their mother. And so did he.

By the time she came home three hours later with a stack of books, a rumpled steno pad and a pencil tucked behind her ear, Darrick was not fit company.

To his further annoyance, she had a way of laying both babies on the old sofa when they wouldn't stop fussying, wrapping her arms around them, and talking on and on at length about the most fantastical things— flowers, fairies, clouds, angels, the moon. And she employed it now with quick success.

The babies stopped crying and stared at her with expressions by which he could now sometimes distinguish them. Michelle was Skye's baby, awed by everything, eyes enormous and mouth always working.

Gabrielle was his—quieter, watchful but less affected by things. Except her mother.

Little legs moved and little arms flailed in uncoordinated patterns as they listened to the sound of Skye's voice.

Without losing the pace of her nonsense tale or changing her tone, she said to him, "Would you bring their bottles, please?" and carried on as they watched her with rapt attention.

"Where's Dori?" he asked, handing her the bottles.

"Still at the library," she returned, in the same musical tone. "She needed more time. I told her I'd pick her up at five-thirty."

She had the twins asleep in fifteen minutes.

Darrick helped her put them down in the crib in the downstairs bedroom that would one day be his parents'. It was now pristine. The day after Tommy's visit, in a fit of ambition, Darrick had buffed all the wide-planked fir floors downstairs, then waxed them that night after Skye had gone to bed. When they'd awakened in the morning, the floors had been dry and gleaming.

The weather had taken a warm turn yesterday morning and Skye had hung a pair of sheer curtains in the bedroom because she said she wanted the babies to see them flutter.

Darrick left the room, intending to head upstairs and go back to the pump roller that he was beginning to feel had grafted itself onto his hip, but Skye stopped him with a hand on his arm.

"You'll never guess what I found!" she said, keeping her voice quiet until they rounded the corner into the kitchen. Then she answered her own question several decibels higher. "Amanda Buckley's cookbook!"

"Who?" he asked, having to dredge up patience when he was certain he hadn't a scrap left.

"Amanda Buckley! Barton Buckley's daughter-in-law. The wife of the man for whom this house was built! And guess what else?"

It was going to involve the mysterious things in the attic, and he didn't want to hear about them now. He was tired and cranky and he wasn't up to listening to ghost stories—or spirit stories.

"Skye, don't be offended," he said, trying to draw away from her, "but if it involves Olivia, I really don't want to hear about it now, okay? I've got lots to do."

"Oh, you do not." With a good-natured grin, she tried to pull him toward the table stacked with books. "You've already done more than anyone could possibly be expected to do in two weeks. And I just wanted to—"

"Skye, I've been listening to babies scream for three hours." He pulled against her again, his voice rising just a little despite his best efforts. "I don't give a rip about Olivia right now and I *don't* want to talk about her."

Skye looked into his eyes and knew the confrontation she'd successfully avoided for several days was now upon her. Darrick, usually the most patient and tolerant of men, was stormy eyed, brick jawed, and looked capable of things she didn't want to think about.

"Is there something you *would* like to talk about?" she asked carefully. The wisest course of action seemed to be to let him ask the questions so that she could assess how much he'd guessed.

"As a matter of fact there is." He walked past her in paint-spattered jeans and sweatshirt to yank open the back door. He stepped out onto the porch, leaned a shoulder against the post and waited for her to join him.

She did, leaving the door open just enough to allow her to hear the babies. "Yes?" she asked.

"Please." He gave her an impatient look and sank down onto the top stair. "Don't give me that quiet and controlled look and manner. I know it isn't real."

She sat beside him, feeling her heartbeat in her throat. "Why do you say that?"

"Because you changed the day you opened the front door and saw Fennerty there." He leaned forward to rest his elbows on his knees and joined his hands as he studied the roll of mountains against the bright blue sky. "You don't look at me the same way. You're afraid now. So don't give me that innocent look."

She turned to him in genuine surprise. "Darrick, you're imagining things. I have never been afraid of you. Why would I be?"

He drew a breath and turned to look at her over his shoulder. His eyes were steady. "Not afraid *of* me. But afraid, maybe, of having to stay with me."

"What?" she demanded. This conversation was taking such a different turn from what she'd expected that she cautioned herself to remain careful. "Darrick, I don't understand."

"Does he want you back?" he asked abruptly.

She was confused by the question. "No. You were standing there when he told us he was getting married."

"You looked unhappy about that."

She probably had. That news had brought back all the dark little memories of their divorce. "I was unhappy about *him!*" she said forcefully. "He was rotten to me, and seeing him standing there in our living room brought it all back."

He considered that, but did not seem convinced. "What was the problem with the two of you?" he finally asked. "You never said."

She rested her forehead in her hands as a means of avoiding his eyes. If he saw guilt in her, he'd suspect she was lying about Tommy.

Tell him now, her conscience prodded her. *It's the perfect moment. He's brought about the confrontation. Be honest and let the chips fall where they may. He loves you. He'll understand and forgive you.*

But the day was so beautiful and so was her marriage to him. She wanted to convince him of her love before she told him of her deceit.

"We'd been friends first," she said truthfully, dropping her hands to her lap and turning to him with a sad smile. "That's supposed to be the perfect prelude to love, but it isn't always. He just one day decided that as a lover I wasn't what he wanted at all."

He still didn't believe her. She was too frustrated to consider that flattering. And now she had to lie. "There was no passion," she went on. "No spark. Maybe love doesn't develop out of friendship. Either it's hot and demanding in the beginning or it just doesn't get there."

He didn't seem convinced by that, either. "When I first met you," he said, "you still wanted him back." It wasn't a question.

She sighed and wondered how someone with a loving family and friends could understand how she'd felt. "I missed the friendship we had," she explained, "not the marriage. In fact, the marriage killed the friendship. Listen to me when I tell you that I haven't given him a thought since the day I moved in with you."

He studied her a moment as though still unsure. "Then why do I see fear in your eyes when you look at me?" he asked insistently.

"Because I *love* you," she said, finding it a relief to be able to be honest again. "And I know what happened the first time. You've been a little impatient with me since Tommy showed up. I guess I've been afraid it could happen to us, too."

And then, like a last-minute rescue, she saw the subtle change take place in his eyes. He believed her. "Skye, that's absurd," he said.

She hooked her arm in his, knowing that there was love in her eyes. "So is the notion that I still have feelings for Tommy when I have you."

His smile was sudden and blinding. She felt relief flood through her followed quickly by an active ripple of guilt she quickly suppressed.

"You have me, all right," he said with rough intensity, taking her into his arms. "God, Skye. You scared me to death."

"I'm sorry," she whispered, kissing the angle of his chin. "But you seemed cross because he'd come, and I thought you were angry about it, so I didn't bring it up when we really should have talked about it."

He threaded his fingers in her hair and kissed her possessively. "I'm sorry, too. Jealousy, sexual frustration and newborn twins are a formula for insanity."

She hugged him tightly. "Well, we'll ask for the same padded cell."

"Funny. Anything else you want to talk about?"

"Yes." She stood and offered him a hand up, eager to put that conversation and the dangers it posed behind them. "I want to tell you about Amanda Buckley. Come on."

Resigned to his fate—actually very pleased with it—Darrick let her lead him inside. She made coffee and opened a package of Mallomars.

She sat across from him at the table, took a cookie and pointed it at the spine of a book halfway down the stack. "Amanda Buckley was apparently quite the hostess and was asked by a local women's group she belonged to to put together some of her recipes into a book for a fund-raising project."

He nodded as he chewed, most of his cookie gone in one bite.

She slid the book from the pile, opened it to a marked page and turned it toward him. "Here! Read this."

He leaned over the old type on the yellowed page and read the line under Skye's pointing finger.

"My elderly aunt in residence with us favors this soup as a remedy for croup." A recipe followed that used chicken stock, vegetables and several other ingredients.

He looked up into Skye's expectant expression, waiting for the connection to dawn on him, but it didn't.

"Her elderly *aunt!*" Skye said emphatically. "I'll bet when Olivia got too old for the Klondike, she came home to Dancer's Beach! She might even have stayed with Amanda—*in this house.*"

"I see." He finally understood. "You think you have an explanation for the bodice thing and why it's here."

She blinked at him and sat up straighter. "Don't you?"

"No," he said with some reluctance, feeling called upon to be logical. "Skye, if the three Buckley brothers married three of the four dancers, then Amanda had at least two aunts by marriage, not counting the ones on her own side of the family. And Olivia didn't marry a Buckley brother, and therefore was not Amanda's aunt."

Skye stared at him, thought it over with turbulent blue eyes, then sagged visibly with disappointment. She rested her elbow on the table and her chin in her hand. With her free arm she reached for the package of cookies and pulled it closer to hold it possessively to her.

"You're not getting another one of these," she said, grimly teasing, "unless you stop undermining my theories."

He leaned against the back of his chair and smiled as he toyed with the handle of his coffee cup. "I've told you before that theories have to be based on fact."

She pointed to the book. "But it says here that her aunt favors…"

"But we've established that she isn't her aunt. And theories should be based on undisputed fact."

She looked stubborn. "I don't believe that. If you had undisputed fact, then you'd no longer have a theory. You'd have a…a…rule, or something."

He had to grant her that. "Okay. You could be right there. But a theory should at least be based on principles that are acknowledged as sound."

She thought that over. "Okay. If you'd acknowledge that my principles are sound, I'd *have* a theory." She smiled tauntingly. "And you'd have a cookie."

Because he'd just endured a day of abject frustration, followed by profound relief, he found her arguments amusing rather than exasperating. And he wanted another cookie.

He took a sip of coffee, folded his arms and slumped thoughtfully in his chair. "Okay. There has to be another way to look at this. I suppose it's entirely possible that an uncle on Amanda's side of the family went to the Klondike looking for gold, met and married Olivia, and if she came home as you theorized, she would be Amanda's aunt."

Skye kept a firm grip on the cookies and shook her head at him. "Now you're making fun of me. What are the chances of that happening?"

Maybe exasperation was going to overtake him after all. "Skye. Sweetie," he said, leaning toward her and doing his best to remain calm. "What are the chances that a woman who's been dead for a hundred years would defy all the laws of science and leave the top of a wedding dress she never wore in the attic of a house she never lived in?"

"One hundred percent," she replied easily. "We have the proof upstairs."

All right, he told himself. You're probably facing a lifetime of just this kind of argument. Be cool. She's right, anyway. That explanation was a little patronizing.

He took another sip of coffee and tried again. "How's this? A lot of children are taught to call friends of the family 'aunt' or 'uncle.' So I suppose

Olivia could have been considered an aunt by the Buckley children and their spouses.''

She liked the notion; he could see it in her eyes. ''But...she left before any Buckley children were born. They wouldn't know her.''

He dismissed that as a problem with a shake of his head. ''She probably sent things home for Christmas and birthdays. She and the other dancers had been through a lot together. I'm sure they wrote and probably exchanged photographs and kept up on each other's lives. They'd have told their children about their experiences and about the romantic figure, Olivia, who'd gone to the Klondike.''

Skye continued to frown for another moment, and Darrick thought his chance at peace—and another cookie—were lost. Then she smiled suddenly and pushed the package of cookies toward him.

''I'll bet that's it!'' she said, clearly pleased with him. ''See? You can be a creative thinker when you put all that undisputed-fact junk aside.''

He winced inwardly at her heresy but took his cookie before she changed her mind. ''It's all in the wrist.''

DARRICK DETECTED LIGHT behind his eyelids, but knew it couldn't be morning. The twins hadn't awakened him yet, and that had to happen at least once, usually twice or even three times before daylight.

So what was it? He forced himself up out of a cozy drowsiness and opened his eyes halfway. He saw an open book illuminated by a shaft of light, and for a moment he thought he might be experiencing some kind of otherwordly visitation by Olivia, who resented his skepticism and intended to frighten him out of it.

Then a hand reached down to the book and turned a page. On the third finger of that hand was a ring he'd put there himself a short time ago.

He slid his head along the pillow until the head bent over the book came into view. All he could see was the shadowy profile. Skye's deep brown hair disappeared into the surrounding darkness.

The sight of her enraptured by whatever she read, her soft cheeks, pert nose and the curly ends of her hair caught in the glow of the flashlight she held over the book all conspired to give a vicious twist to his physical agonies.

"What are you doing?" he demanded sleepily.

"Reading," she replied, sounding distracted. "Guess what I found in the Buckley history?"

He guessed, just to humor her. "Something about Olivia?"

"Sort of." She snuggled closer and tightened her arm around him. "Barton's wife, India, died after they'd been married twelve years. Then guess what Barton did?"

"Buried her, one would presume."

She gave him a light but punitive kick. "After that."

He smiled to himself. "Why don't you just tell me."

"He went to the *Klondike*." She gave his destination reverent emphasis. "The *Klondike,* Darrick."

"To find Olivia, you're thinking."

"Of course." She sighed happily. "Do you see the parallel with us?"

He knew this was going to get him into trouble. "I'm sorry, but I don't."

She propped herself over him with an elbow in his

ribs. "He went to *find* her. Just like you came for me. That's why she left me the bodice. She relates to me."

"Skye…" He was going to try reason one more time, but she chose that moment to kiss him soundly, then flipped off the flashlight, put it and the book aside and snuggled into his shoulder.

"Go to sleep," she admonished. "It's late."

DARRICK AWOKE and found Skye's side of the bed empty. From the kitchen he heard baby sounds and a quiet but urgent conversation. Apparently Dori was up, too.

He showered and dressed and followed the aroma of coffee.

Skye stood at the stove in shorts and a T-shirt, a twin in her arm. He was filled with ambivalent feelings of debilitating tenderness and fierce possession.

Dori carried a twin while she set the table one-handed. She was wearing a dress and looking almost glamorous.

"I'm not nagging," Skye was saying as she turned French toast on the griddle. "I just don't understand what you're being so mysterious about. Do you have a thing for this professor?"

Dori blew air between her lips in a gesture completely at odds with her feminine appearance. "Yeah, right. He's fat and balding and has a passion for marzipan candy. Not my type."

"Then, why does he want to see you?"

"Because he thinks I'm special." Dori hooked her fingers in the handles of a row of three mugs and carried them to the table. "Go figure. He just thought since he's coming to the states to visit his sister, we could get together for a day and go over my thesis outline.''

Skye lifted the edge of one piece of toast to check the underside for doneness. "I thought you were well beyond the outline stage."

"Yeah. So I'd better make sure I'm right before I go any further."

"All right." Skye picked up a pot holder, pulled an empty plate out of the oven and transferred the French toast to it, then put it back. "I'll fly you."

Dori put the last mug in its place with a thunk. "You've spent entirely too much time with my brother. His thick-headedness is rubbing off on you. I'm going to meet the professor *by myself.*" She added emphasis to the last two words. "I'll be back late tonight."

"I'll fly you," Skye bargained, "and we can have time to go shopping before we come back."

"No."

Darrick walked into the room and went to the stove to take the baby from Skye. Skye smiled up at him and lifted her face for his kiss. He loved the easy confidence with which she did that. "Morning," she said.

"Good morning." Dori brought the coffeepot to the table and filled his cup. "I'm going to Seattle today," she said, "and I don't want any arguments about it."

"You don't have to worry," Skye said, putting a plate of French toast in front of him, "because I'm flying her up."

It was time to put his foot down. "No, you're not. I don't like the sound of any of this. I can't believe any professor would make her hang around, waiting for his arrival, then insist she drive a couple of hundred miles to meet him. Neither of you is going. If he's so concerned about her thesis outline, he can come here.''

Dori sat across the table from him with the same look of raging indignation she'd been giving him since she was four. ''Pardon me, but you don't get to pull that on me anymore. I am twenty-three years old.''

''You're also employed by me,'' he said, leaning toward her over his plate, ''at a pretty reasonable salary and for a signing bonus of a top-of-the-line laptop computer. And in the time since we made this deal, you've spent almost a week vacationing with Harper. You go to Seattle and I repo the laptop.''

''Wait a minute.'' Skye sat beside him with a reproachful frown. ''That isn't fair. I know you care about her and worry about her, but she's an adult. She obviously feels this trip is important.''

Darrick turned a warning look on his wife. From what he could tell, it had absolutely no effect.

She looked back at him with an arched eyebrow. ''I also am an adult and perfectly capable of seeing that she remains safely in the company of the professor.''

''Skye…'' Darrick and Dori said hesitantly, but in unison.

Skye patted Darrick's hand. ''I'll call Bertie and ask her if she'll be available to help you with the twins if you need her. Okay?''

''No,'' he replied.

She smiled sweetly. ''Good. I'd better call the field.''

Chapter Eleven

Skye followed Dori into the cab that would take them from Sea-Tac to the Emerald Airport Hotel, grateful that Darrick wasn't here. Dori had been in her own world during the flight, deaf to Skye's questions and attempts at conversation.

And since they'd landed she'd grown pale and had taken on a look of determination that convinced Skye there was something more to this trip than the success of Dori's thesis.

"Why are we booking a room," Skye asked, her trepidation mounting, as Dori presented her American Express and accepted a key card, "when we're leaving tonight?"

Dori caught her arm and pulled her along toward the elevators. "Because those were my instructions," she said quietly. "And please keep your voice down."

"The professor," Skye demanded in a harsh whisper, "asked you to book a room?"

A large group of women in business suits and carrying what appeared to be convention packets poured out of the elevator. Dori tugged Skye onto the car and stabbed the Close Door button before anyone could join them.

When the doors closed, Dori leaned against the railing and heaved a sigh. Then she fixed Skye with a look of grudging amusement. "There is no professor involved here, Skye, and you know it. I can't go into all of it right now. You'll just have to trust me."

Skye was now really glad Darrick wasn't here. "How can I trust you," she asked urgently, "when I don't know what's going on?"

Dori met her gaze. "Because I've known since the day I met you in Mariposa that you're not the twins' mother, but I didn't tell Darrick, did I? I just trusted that your motives weren't intended to hurt. Now you have to trust me."

Skye went still with shock and suspicion. "You mean when you accused me in the kitchen at Edenfield, you...*knew?*"

"Yes, I did."

"You're guessing."

"No—" Dori's gaze was direct "—I know."

Skye still couldn't quite believe it. "Then, why didn't you tell Darrick?"

Dori shrugged. "Because he loves you." Then her jaw firmed and she looked up to watch the floor indicator move from number to number. "And I know who the real mother is, so now that I know love is directing you, I can let you play your little games until you realize what a dangerous thing you're doing."

Skye was caught between utter surprise that Dori had known she was a fake from the beginning and interest in the identity of the babies' real mother.

"Who is Michelle and Gabrielle's mother?" she asked.

Dori shook her head, smoothing the lines of her dress as the elevator settled to a stop on the fourteenth floor. "Can't tell you. But now that you've insisted on involving yourself in this, please just listen and don't say anything. I'll explain what I can on our way home."

Skye was just about to ask what it was she was supposed to listen to when the doors parted to reveal a man standing in the hallway, clearly waiting for them. Skye guessed he was Latino—about Darrick's age—and *handsome* didn't begin to describe him.

He had jet-black eyes, side-parted black hair that was thick and neatly trimmed and a face that was sharply angled and somehow still gorgeous. He wore black slacks, a loose-fitting black shirt and an air of calm authority that Skye noticed even in her complete stupefaction over the day's turn of events.

"Miss Elizabeth Bennet?" the man asked as he put a hand out to hold the elevator door open.

Dori stepped off and pulled Skye with her. "Yes. And this is my sister, Jane."

While Skye did her best to hide surprise and confusion over their sudden aliases, the man studied Dori. Skye thought she saw the barest twitch of his lip.

"I presume you're the demanding Mr. Dominguez." Dori's manner was a little edgy.

Skye wasn't surprised. The man was gorgeous, but looked dangerous. She was suddenly beginning to wish Darrick *was* here.

Dominguez bowed. "I like to think of myself as the *charming* Mr. Dominguez, but whatever you wish. We'll find Mr. Godinez in the room you have just booked at the end of the hall. No, don't ask me how. We have our little tricks." He ushered them ahead of him. "Come. He's eager to meet you."

Skye kept pace with Dori as she marched in the

direction of the door. It was opened by another young man before they reached it, and they were admitted into a typical, high-priced hotel room—everything in beige and white except for colorful silk bouquets on a coffee table and a deep windowsill. Sunny Seattle lay beyond the window, many stories down.

Dori stopped in the middle of the empty room, then turned to confront Dominguez. "Where is he? My sister and I have come a long way and I'm in no mood for games."

Dominguez locked the door behind him, and with a nod of his head, the man who'd admitted them disappeared beyond another door.

"Now, how can you say that," he asked mildly, "when you're clearly playing a masquerade with me?"

Dori's face flushed, though she pretended confusion over the question.

"Elizabeth and Jane Bennet," he clarified without a smile but with a certain pleasure in his eyes in the opportunity to one-up her. "Two of Jane Austen's characters in *Pride and Prejudice.* Never presume, Miss McKeon, that a thief doesn't read."

He did finally smile at her gasp of surprised indignation. "I understand that the ruse was to protect your family from us, but I assure you we represent no threat. Now. I will take your word that you have no weapons on your persons."

Dori rolled her eyes. "Of course we don't. I'm the one who approached you with information, remember? I simply wanted to deliver it over the telephone, but you're the one who insisted I come in person."

Dominguez folded his arms. "Do you give long and complicated answers to *every* question?"

"Just to yours," she replied. "They seem to be required to make sense of the question. Now, may I please see Mr. Godinez?"

He was clearly exasperated with Dori, but there was an interest in his eyes that made Skye think feelingly, *Oh-oh.*

Dominguez opened a connecting door, and Skye and Dori were ushered into a large bedroom that also held a desk and a sofa. A gray-haired man in a paisley silk robe sat at the desk and stood when they entered the room.

He was very tall and appeared robust, though his left arm was in a sling. "Miss McKeon," he said, coming to meet them in the middle of the room and offer his hand. Then he smiled at Skye. "And Mrs. McKeon."

So. Skye didn't know how long Dori had been trying to convince them she was Lizzy Bennet, but she apparently hadn't fooled anyone.

Dori gave Dominguez a dark glance at that. He'd taken a place near the door, and another young man stood by the window, looking out.

"I bring you Julieta's love and good wishes," Dori said, returning her attention to Godinez.

"You are my daughter's confidante?"

"Yes."

The man's expression grew somber. "Then why did she alert the authorities to our business in New Orleans?"

"That wasn't Julie." Dori insisted.

"Only someone privileged to our most intimate plans could have done so."

"That's true. But it wasn't Julie."

He seemed exasperated by her insistence. "Only the

day before, she'd refused to come with us. Pleaded with me to close the family business and berated me when I refused.''

Dori's cheeks flushed and her eyes flashed. ''Your business is thievery, *señor*. She won't live that life anymore. But she loves you. She wanted me to tell you that.''

Godinez swallowed, then demanded, ''If that is true, why have I not seen her in almost a year? Why, when I discovered she'd been hospitalized and came to see her and make peace with her, did she run away from me?''

Skye took in the words and realized that he didn't know his daughter had given birth while in the hospital.

''Because she's in hiding, *señor*,'' Dori replied quietly. ''Since the police have been unable to find you, they are trying to find her, thinking, I'm sure, that she can lead them to you, then be made to testify against you. She obviously doesn't wish to do that. She ran away from you to protect you, Mr. Godinez.''

Godinez caught Dominguez's eye, and they seemed to consider that possibility together. Dominguez came toward them. ''If she establishes a time and place, we can meet her,'' he said.

Dori shook her head. ''That's impossible right now. She's taken a job and another identity to support herself while she tries to determine who *did* betray you.''

''If she came to me,'' Godinez said, his voice suddenly anxious, ''I could protect her.''

''If she came to you, the police would follow. Please. She asks that you let her do this. I will see that no harm comes to her.''

Godinez and Dominguez exchanged that look again,

then Godinez asked with skeptical amusement, "You?"

Dori angled her chin. "I've kept her safe for almost a year. Trust me, please."

Godinez stood. "It isn't that I don't trust you, chica. Simply that I don't trust your body to be as strong as your spirit."

Dori stood also and smiled. "But my brain is, *señor*. And that's what will protect her. I'll be in touch again."

Godinez looked as though he wanted to argue, then finally nodded instead. "Salvatore will take you back to the airport."

Dori headed for the door. "We'll take a cab, thank you."

Dominguez reached it first and placed a hand on the knob. "I will take you," he said politely, but the tone suggested that further argument would be futile.

Dori sighed and nodded. "Very well."

"ARE YOU INSANE?" Skye asked, the moment she'd leveled altitude and speed on the flight back to Edenfield.

Dori was leaning back against her headrest, eyes closed. "As though *your* actions have set a standard for sanity."

Skye frowned at Dori, but Dori missed it. "I'm dealing with a civilized man. You just walked into a den of thieves."

Dori smiled thinly without opening her eyes. "I wouldn't count on Darrick being civilized when the truth comes out," she said. "You just haven't seen him in a temper yet."

"At least he's not hiding from the law!"

"True. But Godinez's daughter is my friend, and she has no one to help her but me."

Skye let a quiet moment pass. "Is it Harper?"

"I told you," Dori reminded her. "I can't tell you any more. Whoever knows her identity is as vulnerable as she is to whoever ratted on the family in the first place."

"*You* know her." Skye grinned in her direction and this time Dori's eyes were open. "And, come on. Let's be honest. Are you really smart enough to keep her and yourself safe?"

Dori shrugged. "I've done it so far."

"Then how come they know who we really are?"

Dori opened her mouth, then closed it again, clearly unable to explain.

"What does Mr. Godinez steal, anyway?" Skye asked.

"Jewels. They're cat burglars."

Skye gasped, then laughed nervously. "You're kidding!"

Dori shook her head. "No, I'm not. He and two sons, Dominguez, who is a nephew, and a couple of friends use the money to support a couple of villages in a poor area of Mexico that neither the government nor the charities ever seem to get to. But it's still stealing."

"My God. A sort of Mexican Robin Hood and his merry band."

"Sort of. Except that it's meant that Julie's lived most of her life in a boarding school, was trained summers and holidays to help out on jobs and finally had to break with her family because she didn't want to spend the rest of her life doing something illegal."

"What happened in New Orleans?"

"Julie had had a fight with her father the night before because she refused to go on the job. When her father and the 'merry band'—" she gave Skye's name for them ironic emphasis "—got to this place in the French Quarter, the police were waiting for them. Mr. Godinez fell and broke his arm, and everybody else took off in different directions. They all got away, but they haven't been able to reconnect yet because the police are still watching. When Julie heard what happened, she went into hiding, knowing the police would come after her to get to her father."

"Does Julie have any idea who told the police about the job?"

"A few, but it's hard to hide out and investigate at the same time. She just got in touch with me about a week ago and asked me to talk to her father. She hated running out on him at the hospital, but she didn't want to risk her father's safety. Or her babies'."

"Geez."

"Yeah. So this is just between us, okay? As far as Darrick knows, we had lunch with my professor and talked about my work."

Skye concentrated on riding out a little turbulence, then frowned at Dori again. "I have one more important question."

Dori turned to look at her.

"Darrick told me I was the only woman he'd been with during the period of time the twins were conceived." She drew a breath, reality beginning to invade after the adventure-novel aspects of that afternoon. "So the babies aren't his, are they?"

Dori lowered her eyes, looking just a little shamefaced. "No."

Skye understood the pain he would feel when he

finally learned that truth, because it had been her pain all along. And it was suddenly easier to blame Dori than it was to blame herself. "You let him believe they were," she accused.

Dori nodded. "It wasn't supposed to happen this way, but Darrick was here, and I knew he'd take good care of the twins and buy Julie some time."

"Then why didn't you just tell him who the real mother is?"

"I told you. Whoever knows is in danger." Dori folded her arms stubbornly. "Nothing's going to happen to this family if I have anything to say about it."

Skye appreciated her noble determination, but couldn't imagine how five-foot, four-inch, one-hundred-eighteen-pound Dori was going to protect everyone.

"The job's getting bigger than you think, Dori," Skye warned.

Dori put a hand to her forehead and closed her eyes again. "Like I hadn't noticed that. Just remember that you're in this with me. I'll keep your secret if you'll keep mine."

Skye had to keep reminding herself of that later that night when she and Darrick lay in their sleeping bag and he asked if everything had truly gone as well as Dori had insisted it had earlier.

"Beautifully," she lied. "Her professor's a very nice man and seemed very interested in her thesis."

"So she's on the right track?"

"Ah...yeah. Right track."

"And you?"

"Me?"

"You. You look a little pale. You feel tense." He

tightened his grip on her in the darkness. "You're not having second thoughts about Tommy?"

She pinched his side, and he pulled her hand away with an emphatic "Ouch!"

That seemed to satisfy him as a reply. In a few moments he was asleep and she was left to stare into the darkness and grieve over everything she would surely lose when Darrick learned the truth. The babies. Him.

SKYE STOOD face-to-face with Olivia in the attic. She wasn't literally face-to-face, she was forced to remind herself, but rather face to bodice, yet she felt the dancer's presence as though the dress form had been replaced by her person.

Skye put a fingertip to the tiny ruffle of chiffon that would have framed a delicate chin and imagined the pretty woman with a dancer's body who'd dreamed of wearing the dress.

"I'm sorry you couldn't have babies," she told her, her own sadness sitting like a truck on her chest. "I'm sorry Barton chose to marry India and that your life was ruined." She took hold of the yellowed sleeves with their jeweled points at the wrist and held them out. "Did you send this to me? Or better yet, did you bring it?" She looked around at the clean and bare attic in which there was no place for a person to hide—at least not one with a physical body.

There was banging overhead where Darrick worked on the roof, and a cozy silence from the hallway just below the attic stairs where she'd left the sleeping babies in a carrier. Dori had walked to the library again.

Though Skye had no idea what a spirit might sound

like if it replied to her question, she listened for some sign of a presence. But all she heard was Darrick.

She let the sleeves fall and sighed, wondering if guilt was making her crazy.

She ran a hand lovingly over the beading that led to a V at the waist, then turned to the stairs. She sat on the floor at the edge of the hole and lowered her legs to connect a foot with a rung of the ladder.

And then she heard the sound. It was just a faint rush of air, a bare disturbance of the atmosphere, almost like a breath drawn or expelled.

The fine hairs raised on her arms, and her heart punched against her rib cage as she turned to look.

"Olivia?" she whispered.

Then she realized that there was nothing solid under the foot on which she'd shifted her weight and she was falling...falling.

DARRICK WAS HALFWAY down the ladder outside when he heard the crash. He'd left the front door open to the sunny day when he'd hauled out the ladder and he shouted toward it.

"Skye?"

He proceeded down the ladder at a normal pace, expecting any moment to hear her reply that she was all right, that she'd dropped something, or that the horse-collar clock had fallen despite its sturdy molly screws.

But she didn't respond.

He walked into the quiet living room and shouted her name again, sure she simply hadn't heard him.

"Skye!" he shouted.

When there was still no answer, he began to feel a vague unease.

He hurried through the dining room into the empty kitchen, still calling her name. "Skye? Skye!"

The house was eerily quiet, just the sound of the surf at the front of the house, and birdsong and a breeze in the trees when he opened the back door to see if she'd gone out to collect honeysuckle.

There was no sign of her. Concern was rapidly turning to fear. He ran up the stairs to the second floor. His eyes fell on the carrier first, the sleeping babies in it, then on the crumpled figure in jeans and a sweatshirt beside it, one harm hooked on the bottom rung of the ladder to the attic.

Fear threatened to become panic.

He said her name as he fell to his knees beside her, carefully touching the arm on the rung, feeling for broken bone. "Skye? Are you all right? Can you talk to me?"

She groaned and raised her free arm to her head. "Darrick?" she asked, her voice raspy and stunned. "What happened?"

He cupped her head in his hand, gently freed her arm from the ladder and eased her back onto the floor.

"I think you fell," he said, hearing the tremor in his voice as he tore off his sweatshirt and balled it under her head. "Don't budge!" he ordered as he leaped to his feet. "I'm going to call an ambulance."

She winced. "I'm okay, I think," she said thickly, uncertainly. "Just...give me a minute."

But he was already at the phone, dialing 911.

He saw Skye off in the ambulance over her insistence that she was sure she hadn't broken anything, then took the twins to the Fishers.

"Of course we'll watch them!" Bertie said, taking the carrier from him, her expression filled with concern and kindness. "Do you want Cliff to drive you to the hospital?"

Cliff took the diaper bag Darrick handed him and already had car keys out.

"Thanks, but I'm fine." He backed onto the porch, eager to follow Skye. "She was talking, and she insists she's all right, but it was quite a fall. There are diapers and bottles in there…" He pointed to the bag Cliff held. "I don't know how long I'll be, but I'll call you from the hospital."

Bertie shooed him away. "Don't worry about us, we're good at this. Go."

Darrick drove to the hospital in Lincoln City on automatic pilot, some heavenly radar guiding his conformity to traffic safety. His mind was preoccupied with thoughts of how necessary Skye had become to his existence, how desperate he'd felt when he'd found her crumpled on the floor in the upstairs hallway, how wrong it was at this moment to have their little family separated with her in the hospital, him on the road, and their babies with the Fishers.

All he could do, he thought, was pray that Skye was as fine as she claimed to be, and that they would all be reunited in a couple of hours.

There was not a soul in the Emergency Room waiting area. A smiling clerk greeted him and told him that Skye had been taken to Radiology.

"How was she when she came in?" he asked.

The young woman smiled. "Insisting that she was fine," she said, "and that we make sure you were informed of that when you arrived. The doctor tried to tell her that he should be the one to make that evaluation, but she made me promise that I would tell you *she* was sure she was fine. Then she asked me to buy you these.''

She handed him a box of Raisinettes. "There are more in the candy machine in the hallway if this isn't enough.'' Though he guessed she was younger than he, her expression became maternal. "She says they have a calming effect on you.''

He felt touched and tortured at the same time. He closed his hand around the box, remembering the first one he and Skye had ever shared.

"Jelly beans do it for me,'' the clerk went on. "Not a healthy raisin in the whole bag. Before you sit down, Mr. McKeon, could you help me with something?''

He drew a breath and tried to relax. "Sure. What is it?''

"I've been trying to get Valley Memorial to fax your wife's records to us, but they can't locate her file. I do have the right hospital?''

Ah, yes. She'd had the babies under a phoney name. "Try under Rachel Whitney,'' he said.

The clerk's eyes widened. "An...alias?''

He smiled, a little high on relief now that he was at least in the same building with Skye. "She's a spy,'' he whispered.

The clerk gasped, then decided she was being teased and shook her head. "And to think I bought you a box of Raisinettes.''

He reached into his pocket for a bill, but she stopped him with a raised hand and a grin. "Never mind. It was a dull afternoon. Have a seat.''

Twenty minutes later a stocky, gray-haired doctor came through the Emergency Room doorway and Darrick rose to greet him.

"Mr. McKeon," the doctor said, offering his hand. "I'm Hal Binford."

"How is she?" Darrick demanded as he shook his hand.

"A little banged up." The doctor led him back to the sofa and sat down with him. He grinned. "That's a technical diagnosis. She'll have a few bruises, probably lots of soreness, but she was right. She hadn't broken anything."

Darrick felt the knot of worry in his stomach dissolve into relief that spread throughout his body. He drew another deep breath. "She fell straight down out of an attic. I can't believe nothing's broken."

The doctor nodded. "Me, either. The EMTs told us you were worried about her arm because she'd caught it on the rung of the ladder, but it seems to be all right, too. Not even sprained. She was lucky."

Darrick realized that he was, too. "Can she go home now?"

The doctor nodded, then leaned toward Darrick as though not quite finished with what he had to say.

Darrick focused on him, all senses suddenly alert. Something *was* wrong.

"She's getting dressed right now," Doctor Binford said, his brow furrowed, "but I wanted to verify something with you." He lowered his voice as the clerk chatted cheerfully on the telephone. "I asked Valley Memorial to check this and they did—twice. But it still doesn't make sense. I understand you're the administrator there."

"Yes."

"Well…" The doctor shifted uncomfortably. "First of all, there's the fact of your wife's file being under a different name."

"Yes." Great, Darrick thought. Skye's fine but now we're going to be arrested for what the hospital is bound to think is some kind of fraud. "It's her middle name and maiden name," he lied with a smile. "We weren't married when she delivered the babies, she thought I didn't care, and she was hiding from me."

The doctor studied him closely, suspiciously, then looked down at the file in his hands. "If that's true, how do you explain that Rachel Whitney has a different blood type than your wife, and is three inches shorter?"

Darrick stared at him, unable to make sense of the question. "What?" he asked finally.

"Rachel Whitney was five feet three inches tall," he said reading from the file, "and O negative. Your wife is five foot seven, and B positive."

Darrick wished desperately that he could do something other than stare. But though his brain worked furiously, he could think of nothing to explain...

"And just for what it's worth," the doctor continued, "she has a remarkably muscular abdomen for a woman who's delivered twins so recently. And none of the stretch marks. You said she was hiding from you. Did you see her during her pregnancy? Were you...present for the births?"

The explanation was coming at Darrick like a bullet in slow motion. He could see its approach, understand completely what it would do to him when it hit, know instinctively he might not survive. He put a hand to the back of a chair.

It hit him with the impact of a loaded log truck. Everything inside him vibrated with the pain. Skye had lied. She had not given birth to the twins. "You weren't?" the doctor asked, standing also.

Darrick spun on him, shock and anger warring for control of his emotions. He reminded himself that this wasn't the doctor's fault.

"No, I wasn't," he replied in slim control of his voice. "She delivered early and I was...at a conference."

The doctor pointed toward the ER door. "But that is your wife?" He was beginning to look a little panicky himself. "We are talking about the same woman?"

He couldn't relate the pain he felt to anything else. It was sharper than a stab wound, hotter than a burn, deeper than an internal injury.

For a minute it was all he could do to remain standing.

Then he reminded himself that he couldn't be absolutely certain of what happened until he heard it from Skye herself.

He pulled himself together and nodded at the doctor. "We are talking about the same woman. I'd like to take her home now."

The doctor looked at him as though he wanted very much to ask him to explain. But instead he replied courteously, "Come on back and we'll see if she's ready."

SKYE READ THE TENSION in Darrick's face the moment he walked into the room. She wrapped her arms around him, touched by it and wanting to soothe it away.

"I'm okay," she said, holding him tightly. "Just bruised and...sore."

She felt the stiffness in him and stepped back, smiling, prepared to tell him again that she was fine. Then she saw in his eyes that the visible strain actually concealed a cold, deep anger.

She studied it in momentary surprise. Then she realized what it signified, and all the warmth left her body in a sudden rush. His stare froze her to the spot.

He knew she'd lied about being the twins' mother.

She wanted to die, but she'd just been declared in relatively good health considering the fall off the ladder.

So she tried to call her thoughts into order, to put together a coherent explanation that Darrick would understand and possibly even sympathize with.

But her brain didn't seem to be able to come up with anything but panic, self-recriminations and regret. And Darrick didn't look capable of sympathy at the moment.

Her mind in a fog, she pretended to pay attention as the doctor spoke to Darrick, handed him a prescription, gave him some instructions.

Then the doctor waved them off, and Skye walked through the open ER door, then out the front door to the Lexus in the parking lot.

Darrick unlocked her door with the remote and walked around to the driver's side without helping her in, a courtesy he always accorded her.

Not that she'd needed that little slight to understand that he was furious.

He was sitting behind the wheel before she even had her door open. Her head pounding and her heart a lead weight in her chest, Skye climbed into the passenger seat, pulled her door closed and buckled her seat belt.

Darrick's fury was a palpable thing. She turned to look at him but he was staring through the windshield, his profile looking as though it had been quarried. His wrist rested on the top of the steering wheel, his hand in a fist.

"I can explain," she said, her voice quiet and gravelly. She hadn't swallowed in the past several minutes.

"So you're *not* the twins' mother." It was a statement made in a voice almost as quiet as hers, but it had a furious edge to it.

After the last three weeks, it was so hard to say the word. "No," she admitted, having to force the word out. And still it was almost soundless.

He turned to her, a punitive anger in his eyes. "I didn't hear you." But she knew he was simply making her say it again to hurt her. She accepted that as fair.

"No," she said more firmly. "I didn't give birth to the twins."

He put the key in his fist in the ignition and turned it.

"Where are they?" she asked him over the sound of the motor.

He ignored her, backed out of the parking spot and headed for the exit to the street. He pulled up at the stop sign and waited for the traffic to pass.

She took that moment to put a cautious hand to his arm. "Darrick, where are—"

He shook her hand off without turning to her, as though he didn't trust himself to look at her. "Don't touch me," he said, his voice low and fierce, "and don't talk to me until we get home."

"All right," she agreed, "but tell me where the girls are."

"It doesn't matter," he said, his manner changing from rage to grim control as he turned the car onto the street. "We've just established that they're not yours."

She held herself together through most of the ride home by trying to analyze where he could have taken the babies with Dori at the library. The choices were slim. He could have taken them to the Fishers, or if they weren't home, to Polly's office.

She'd probably lost them forever now, she realized, but found some comfort in the black hole that had suddenly become her life by knowing where they were.

She imagined them together in their carrier, tiny fingers entwined as they slept. Then pain caught her in a mighty fist and shook her until her heart broke.

"They're at Cliff's and Bertie's," Darrick said as they entered the outskirts of Dancer's Beach.

It wasn't until she heard the sound of his voice that she became aware of her own sobs.

He parked in front of the drugstore across the street from the hotel. He ripped the prescription out of his pocket and left the car. Skye took advantage of the time he was gone to cry her heart out.

He was back in ten minutes then drove silently home. In the house he barged past a surprised-looking Dori and went straight to the kitchen and called the Fishers.

Dori, at the table with books spread out over it, looked at Skye and guessed that Darrick knew. Skye could read it in her face.

"We're home," Darrick said into the phone, "but Skye is a little…yes, she's going to be fine, but she's a little banged up. Are the girls making you crazy yet?" He listened for a moment, and Skye could hear Bertie's excited voice answering his question.

"Good," he said when she stopped. "Then would you mind watching them for another hour so I can…get Skye comfortable? Great. Thanks, Bertie. Right. I'll tell her."

Darrick hung up the phone, then turned to Dori. "Could you go upstairs please, Dori. We need privacy."

"Darrick…" Dori looked from one to the other in concern.

"It's all right," Skye told her.

"I…" Dori began, prepared, Skye guessed, to take the blame for her part in the deceit.

"No," Skye interrupted her, telling her firmly with her eyes to be quiet. "Excuse us, Dori."

Dori walked toward the stairs, casting a worried look over her shoulder.

Darrick pulled a bottle of pills out of his pocket and slapped it on the counter.

Skye's head now thudded viciously, but she ignored the prescription for pain. She needed her wits about her to try to explain her actions to Darrick.

So she filled the kettle instead.

Darrick backed into the corner of the counter farthest away from where she stood. He folded his arms and indicated the prescription with a jut of his chin. "The doctor said to take one of those when you got home."

There was no kindness in his voice, Skye noted, just the stiff recitation of fact.

She reached overhead for a pair of mugs and placed them on the counter, then turned to face him. It hurt to look at him because she could see beyond the angry and arrogant set of his jaw to the pain in his eyes. Pain she had put there.

She didn't bother to wonder how she could have done this. She'd known in the beginning that it wouldn't work for long, yet she'd opted to do it for the time it would allow her. She'd considered that time spent as Darrick's wife and the twins' mother would be worth the ultimate separation and loneliness discovery would bring.

"Yes, I know," she said, standing stiffly beside the counter, a hand on the cold tile for support. "But they'll make me feel woozy and I...want to talk to you first."

He said nothing encouraging, simply stood there, staring at her with those hurt and angry eyes, waiting for her to go on.

She drew a breath and found that it hurt. Everything hurt suddenly—her head, her ribs, her stomach, her side. But she ignored her body's discomfort and tried to find a way to explain.

"The time we spent on the mountain after the crash," she said, pushing away the warm memories so that she could think clearly and so she could save them from the contamination of the moment, "was the most...wonderful twenty-two hours of my life... except for the last three weeks."

"That must be why you returned my calls so promptly." His voice was chillingly neutral.

Her throat was beginning to constrict, and she had to swallow to be able to keep talking. "I explained that in part." She had to swallow again. "My family..."

He nodded. "I know. Dysfunctional and cold. But the world's full of people who've suffered. It doesn't give them an unlimited credit line for cruelty."

She met his eyes. "You're absolutely right. But it

makes them a little more desperate to reach for happiness when they find it.''

He studied her coldly. ''You're saying that in your desperate reach for happiness, you felt entitled to incinerate mine and the babies' by pretending to be what you weren't?''

''No,'' she denied quietly, trying to remember how she'd felt that afternoon at the airport. It seemed like an eternity ago. ''But when you came to Mariposa, you were so convinced that I was the mother.''

''You came running to the twins!'' he said, straightening out of his relaxed pose, his voice rising. ''You looked so happy to see them. I thought...''

''I *was* happy to see them,'' she tried to explain. ''I love babies.''

''But you told me they were yours!''

''You told me they were mine!'' she shouted, then finished lamely, ''I just agreed with you because I wanted them to be.''

''And you think that excuses you?'' His hot question filled the kitchen.

She was almost relieved to see his cold anger ignite.

''I'm not trying to excuse myself,'' she replied. ''Just to explain. A husband and children were what I've wanted all my life, and when you presented me with the opportunity to reach out and take it...'' Her throat closed again and her eyes welled with tears. ''I did,'' she finished in a frail voice.

He spread his arms in helpless frustration. ''You just said you didn't return my calls because you thought your background prevented you from being able to be part of a family.''

''I did,'' she returned reasonably, ''but it didn't stop me from wanting that.''

"Then wouldn't the logical course of action be to find someone with whom you felt compatible and see what happened, rather than tell a lot of lies and steal someone else's life?"

She nodded, suddenly impervious to all the other hurtful things that happened in her life. This moment far outdistanced any of those.

"I tried that with Tommy Fennerty."

His anger subsided fractionally, but his expression didn't change. "Marriages that don't work are a fairly common occurrence. That doesn't mean—"

"Oh, it worked," she corrected him. "What I told you before wasn't true. We were very happy in every way. Then I had a ruptured appendix on a hiking trip. We'd walked a day and a half into the woods, and by the time Tommy got me back and into a hospital, peritonitis had set in and I was...sterilized."

She heard a scream and thought it was in her own mind. Then she realized it was the kettle and turned off the burner and moved the kettle onto a cold one.

"Anyway," she went on, "Tommy's from a big Irish family with lots of children, and he finally admitted that he didn't think he could deal with being unable to have his own. So he left."

Sun streamed through the windows as the kitchen rang with silence. Skye chanced a look up at Darrick and found him staring at the floor.

He looked up at her, his eyes grim, his expression only slightly softened.

"I'm sorry," he said. "I'm sure that was awful for you."

"The thing was..." She reached for the box of tea on the counter, but held it to her without opening it while she struggled to explain the conclusion she'd drawn from that experience. "I thought if my sterility got that reaction from my own husband with whom I'd been friends for ages, and with whom I'd shared a really good marriage for a year and a half—then there was little chance I'd ever find a man who could deal with it. So I had just resigned myself to living my life around my flight service."

She opened the box of tea and put a bag in each cup. The aroma of bergamot rose to give her a tiny fragment of pleasure.

"Then you came along." She closed the box and put it back, then turned to him, feeling a weird calm overtake her. There was something very settling, she thought absently, about having nothing left to lose. "We had that wonderful night, you kept calling me, and the sound of your voice and my memories completely destroyed the comfortable, if empty, little life I'd been willing to settle for." She looked him in the eye. "You made me want all those things I'd accepted I would have to live without. But I didn't return your calls because I wanted you to be able to find some other young woman who could give you children to fit into your wonderful family."

Darrick wondered what it was about this woman that always made him feel as though he was dying. First with sexual frustration, then with the fear of losing her, now with emotions so conflicted that a polarity storm roared in his insides.

She'd done a cruel and selfish thing to him that had made him only minutes ago want to throw her out of his life. But now as she explained her motives, he was still enraged, yet at the same time something inside him was trying to make him understand. He tried to turn it off, not wanting to.

"You had a pretty small opinion of my character," he said.

"Not at all," she denied. "I had a high opinion of what I wanted you to have. All the things I knew I couldn't give you."

"And what did you think entitled you to make decisions for me?"

"Love." She replied without even taking a moment to think. Her eyes were wide and direct as they looked into his. "You were everything I thought didn't exist for me—kindness, laughter, a protective courtesy I was sure had long since been bred out of the world's male gene pool."

Sympathy rose in him, but he tamped it down. "And that's why, when the opportunity to ruin my life presented itself, you took it?"

Large tears slid down her cheeks but she brushed them away and tossed her head. He had to look away from the sunshine rippling in her hair.

"I can't deny that at the bottom of everything, my motives were selfish." Her mouth began to quiver, but she put a hand to it and drew a deep breath. "But the babies' mother had *left* them, and there *you* were, just as I remembered you, and…"

He heard one sob, then she sniffed, lowered her hand to her pocket and squared her shoulders. He steeled himself against her look of misery.

"I calmly calculated my options," she admitted with a candor he grudgingly admired, "and considered that it was a terrible thing to do to you, but if I was able to make you love me before you found out the truth, then you'd be able to forgive me, and I'd spend the rest of my life making you glad that you did."

She paused to draw a breath and struggled against

a resurgence of emotion. ''Or,'' she continued, ''you would just hate me and I would be...gone.''

''But you must have thought that wouldn't really happen if you took the chance.''

''But I did,'' she said with grim dignity. ''I knew that however it worked out, I'd have a couple of weeks with you. And that was worth everything.'' Then she smiled sadly. ''You told me your brothers and Dori were haunted by Donovan's death, but you weren't sure how it had affected you. Well, I think I know. It's made you need to understand everything, to force it to make sense. I suppose because that's the only way a child could deal with something so terrible. But I don't think things always do make sense—I think love defies reason.'' Her voice lowered to a whisper. ''And I do love you.''

Darrick stared at her as she watched him, her eyes hopeful of any small measure of understanding. She looked fragile in the beam of sunlight with all her makeup gone and her hair and clothes disheveled.

If he put aside his own considerable pain and sense of betrayal, he was able to understand what had prompted her. And in all fairness, he had to admit that she'd been a completely devoted wife and mother in their short time together.

But at the moment he *wasn't* able to put his own feelings aside. And even if he did understand her, he couldn't forgive her.

''You think the twins will understand?'' he asked brutally.

Her lips trembled again and her misery deepened. He hated himself, but for now he hated her, too.

''What you're missing here,'' he said, fury rolling in him anew, ''is that if they're not yours, they're not mine, either! They're Dillon's or Duncan's, but they're not *mine!* Your intention might have been to put together a happy little family for yourself, but it was my family, too! And now it isn't anymore!''

Unable to bear another moment of the unhappiness generated between them, he stormed out to the car.

Chapter Twelve

Skye awoke to the sound of babies crying. She was out of the sleeping bag and all the way to the bedroom door before reflex gave way to coherent thought and she remembered that her assistance wouldn't be welcome.

She heard Dori offer to help, Darrick's dismissing voice, then Dori's retreat up the stairs.

Darrick's deep voice continued as he tried to soothe the twins. She wondered how long the three of them had been up. The cries had a weary sound, as though it had been a while.

Skye stood uncertainly in the doorway and put a hand to her head. Her thoughts still felt a little thick, rather than sharp and clear, and she guessed the medication hadn't quite worn off yet.

The crying softened slightly, and she smiled wistfully in the darkness at the pattern she now recognized. Gabrielle had fallen asleep, but Michelle always needed extra crying time to be able to settle down sufficiently to sleep.

Skye went back to her lonely sleeping bag, knowing Darrick could handle the baby. He had the patience of Job and would soon have Michelle asleep.

When fifteen minutes had passed and Michelle continued to cry, Skye sat up and reassessed the situation. Darrick was skilled and calm with the twins, but then he'd had one hell of a day today. It was possible Michelle was picking up the tension in him and that was feeding her naturally high-strung nature.

Unable to listen to the sound a moment longer without trying to do something about it, Skye got to her feet and marched resolutely to the kitchen where only the small light over the stove was lit.

Darrick was pacing toward the back door with the baby. Skye stopped in the doorway and felt a deep pang at the sight of the screaming baby on his shoulder. Not a romantic picture, she knew, but when this was over that was how she would think of him with his long, hard body she'd had the privilege of knowing only once, tenderly accommodating the baby, who clung to him in the strange and confusing first weeks of life.

They hadn't talked about the disposition of their relationship yet and that was fine with her. She knew the only outcome possible, and she'd just as soon not hear it spoken aloud until the last possible moment.

Darrick reached the door and turned, then stopped when he saw her. It took him only a moment to look her over in grim silence.

"What do you want?" he asked as he continued to pace.

"I thought you might need a little help." She took several steps toward him but he changed direction.

She stopped where she stood with a sigh.

"Thanks, but I'll manage," he said.

"But you should get some rest. Your parents will be here in a couple of days." He made a scornful sound she took to mean he thought there was little chance he'd be able to sleep even if he had the opportunity.

"They called while you slept," he said as he stopped at the back door and turned. "They'll be here in the afternoon, day after tomorrow." He raised his voice to be heard over the crying baby. "When they've all had a great time and are ready to go home, you can explain your scheme and what it's going to mean to them. Then we're quits."

He spoke grimly, but she thought she saw a chink in the armor of his anger, a flare of fear in his eyes when he added that last sentence. Perhaps she had imagined it, but she didn't think so. She watched him hopefully for another sign.

"We'll have to get a bed for your parents," she said.

"I know. That's not a problem."

He turned again in his pacing before he reached touching distance of her, no sign of another chink even remotely visible.

Skye decided to try to make her own. She'd gotten into this with a certain fearless determination to put to good use whatever time was allowed her. She may as well go out of it the same way.

"Oh, for heaven's sake," she said, taking several quick steps after him and turning him around. "Give her to me."

He held the baby away. "You have no right," he began in a superior tone.

She pried the baby out of his arms. "I have as much right as you have. And if you're going to be rigid with anger for the next week, both babies are going to be screaming every time you touch them."

"Well, forgive me if I'm rattled by what you've done!"

Skye placed the baby right over her breasts and held her tightly as she rocked from side to side.

"I know you have every right to be," she said reasonably. The baby's cries diminished almost instantly. "I just mean that everyone's going to have a miserable weekend if you don't let some of the anger go."

He rotated a stiff shoulder then filled a cup with water and put it in the microwave. "I'm sure that'd be more comfortable for you," he said, turning to face her.

Soft little whimpery sounds now issued from the baby. Skye met Darrick's eyes. "I assure you that nothing in my life is comfortable now, nor is it likely to be again. After Memorial Day, I'll have to live without you. You'll be pleased to know that that'll be hell."

Michelle was asleep.

Sometime during the night, Darrick had moved the portable crib out of the bedroom where Skye had slept and placed it in the living room near the sofa, where a rumpled blanket lay in one corner.

"Good night," she said, and went to place Michelle beside Gabrielle. She adjusted blankets, touched tiny fingers and took a moment to utter a prayer over them that the woman who ultimately became their mother would love them as much as she loved them.

She ran to the bedroom and closed the door.

DARRICK PREPARED for his family's arrival with the feeling that the Fates had bent his reality. Many of the elements in it remained the same, but everything had a slightly different aura, a different texture, a different meaning.

The twins, for example.

Suddenly, the day following Skye's fall—and he laughed about it wryly when he referred to it that way because in his life the sky had indeed fallen—Michelle and Gabrielle learned to smile.

He thought it ironic that such a momentous event happened at such a time, but it did lighten his mood. He even wondered if the babies had conspired to do it as a way to take some of the heat off of Skye. They smiled at the sight of her, at the sound of her voice, and when she picked them up.

And the first time they smiled for him he felt as though his purpose on earth had been established. And though the knowledge that they weren't his babies hurt abominably, he found comfort in the fact that they did belong to one of his brothers. At least he was the twins' uncle and could remain in their lives.

His sister was behaving strangely. She was solicitous of him and protective of Skye. For someone who'd once been suspicious of Skye's intentions, she now couldn't do enough for her, even though her suspicions had proven to be well-founded.

Then there was his wife.

The warm, loving woman who'd lived with him for three weeks looked superficially the same.

She did all the things she'd done for him before— cooked, helped paint, massaged his overworked muscles, and did her best to see that he was comfortable.

But her eyes withheld the intimacy he used to so enjoy seeing there. And except for the back rubs, she kept a careful distance from him.

It was as though she'd relegated herself to the position of friend. Despite the embers of anger that remained in him, he missed the easy affection they'd shared and the touch of her hand and her lips that had always brought him such comfort.

And his libido was more of a problem than ever.

Skye had lied to him, deceived him and made him look like an idiot to the doctor at the Lincoln City hospital.

But now when he looked at her, the fact often uppermost in his mind was that she *hadn't* recently delivered twins and that he could make love to her if he was so disposed.

He reminded himself repeatedly that he wasn't so disposed. Sex had never guided his actions and wouldn't now, no matter how long he'd been deprived of it. But the sight of her in shorts and T-shirts, and in the oversize shirt she wore at night, was making him mad with longing.

It all became unbearable the day they shopped for a bedroom set for his parents' room. Dori had errands to run in town and volunteered to care for the twins while Darrick and Skye shopped.

So they'd shopped unhindered by carriers and diaper bag.

He'd headed for an oak set and Skye was drawn to a natural wicker one. He followed because he was drawn to her, a phenomenon he couldn't explain in light of what she'd done to him.

"This looks beach-housey, don't you think?" she asked, inspecting the two wicker bedside tables, each with a small storage shelf underneath.

"Beach-housey?" he repeated after her. He pulled open a dresser drawer and was pleased to see that it had metal slides. "Is that a decorating term?"

She made a face at him. "You know what I mean. It's light and airy and looks appropriate to a beach house." Then she pointed to the light oak set that had caught his attention. "Of course that would, too, in a more formal way. What kind of furniture do your parents have at home?"

He had to think. "Old maple stuff. Used to be Grandma Beale's set. You're thinking they'd want something completely different when they come to the beach?"

She shrugged a shoulder. "That's logical. But you know them better than I."

She was stepping back into what she'd decided was her "place," and though he was willing to admit that everything he'd said to her the day the sky fell probably encouraged such an action, he was growing more and more impatient with her doing it.

That was something else he didn't understand and couldn't explain.

They decided on the wicker set, then tried out mattresses and pillows when a well-meaning clerk all but pushed them side by side onto a medium-soft mattress, then placed one long, single, goose down pillow under their heads. Darrick reached the limit of his endurance.

Had there been government secrets at stake, he'd have divulged them; a list of covert operatives, he'd have given them up. He'd been tortured to the breaking point.

Thanks to small-town efficiency, they were able to purchase bedding in the same shop, and the delivery truck followed them home with all their purchases.

They'd arrived home to a note from Dori that said she and the twins had been invited to tea.

Darrick was determined to remain in the doorway

and simply watch as Skye made up the bed, but all the walking around and back-and-forth adjustment of the sheets called for another pair of hands, and he went in to help her.

"I think they'll like this," she said, handing him a pillow cover. "And I love the tropical colors in the bedding. I swear if you sat in this room long enough, you could hear macaws and kettle drums."

He stuffed the pillow into the brightly flowered case, then shook it until it settled. "I don't think macaws and kettle drums come from the same place."

She fluffed her pillow into place and scolded in a gently, friendly voice, "You're so literal. I was going for tropical ambience."

She reached over to fluff his pillow after he placed it, and he drank in the expanse of bare midriff and the length of leg kicking out behind her.

Then she pulled the bulky coverlet out of a bag and dropped it in the middle of the bed. Together they unfolded it, being absurdly careful not to bump hands, then stretched it out over the sheets.

She walked around to his side to measure the length of coverlet hanging down, tugged on it such an infinitesimal amount that he thought it hardly seemed worth the effort, then tucked in the top and worked the slack under the pillows.

She stood back to admire their work.

"Do you like it?" she asked him.

"Yes, I do," he said. It was bright and cheerful in the white room—and definitely beach-housey. "It was a good choice."

"Needs flowers," she declared and shot past him through the kitchen and out into the backyard.

He went to the bedroom window and watched her

cut honeysuckle and a pink, gangly flower that grew wild along the fence. The clutch of flowers in hand, she headed back toward the door, but stopped suddenly in the middle of the yard.

She looked up at the sky for a moment, then at the yard around her with a kind of fatalistic slope to her shoulders. Then she put the flowers to her nose and started slowly toward the door.

When she came back into the room with the flowers in a water glass and a coaster to put them on, her lips were smiling but her eyes were not.

She put the glass on the dresser and looked around her, a subtle shift visible in her mood.

"We should have thought about lamps for the bedside tables," she said.

"Those will be easy enough to find."

She went to the window and opened it slightly. The day was warm, the air fragrant, and the late afternoon breeze blew the curtains in so that they fluttered and swirled as though the wind wore them.

Love raged in him.

He knew that was a ridiculous thought. Love didn't rage. But when a man felt it when he didn't want to, when he had grievances and grudges he couldn't put aside but brimmed with romantic emotions anyway, his heart was at war.

Skye went toward the sleeping bags he'd kicked into a corner when the bed was moved in. But he stood between her and them. And she'd been making a point of staying beyond his reach.

She stopped several feet from him, expecting him to move.

He knew he should. But he couldn't. He was beginning to tremble inside with the angry love in him.

He stood squarely in her path and stretched his hands out toward her.

She glanced at them suspiciously, then looked up at him with wary eyes. But she put her hands in his.

He drew her closer, almost as an experiment for his own benefit, trying to decide which emotion was uppermost. If anger predominated, this would be a bad idea.

But he reacted to her the same way he had ten months ago when they'd huddled together under the same tarpaulin. He wanted to hold her, not hurt her.

He looped his arms around her and lowered his head to kiss her.

Skye stood absolutely still, afraid of disturbing the fragile emotional ecology that had brought her to this moment. She'd dreamed of it over the past few days, alternately prayed for it and given up on it.

She'd hurt him too deeply and too horribly.

And she felt some of his anger when his mouth opened on hers. He was tender and gentle, but there was a tension in him that had never been present when he touched her. She guessed that meant the tenderness wasn't a natural impulse, but a deliberate one.

So she offered him her own, putting her hand to his cheek and straining up to him, moving her lips on his with the love and trust that had led her into his life in the first place.

His hand in the middle of her back pressed her closer to him. She enjoyed the breathless confinement as he deepened the kiss, his shoulders, chest, arms forming a safe harbor for her after the cold, dark isolation of the past few days.

He trailed kisses from her jaw to her ear, along her throat to the shirt buttons just above her breasts.

Then he raised his head and looked into her eyes, his expression both turbulent and tender. "I want to make love to you," he said.

She wanted that more than anything, but there was a clear conflict in him that concerned her. She forced herself to think.

"Out of revenge?" she asked.

"No," he replied. "Out of love."

She blinked at him, surprised. "Then you've forgiven me?"

He looked at her for a long moment, then he held her gaze and answered honestly, "No. I want to. I think I even understand somewhat. But…that's as far as I can go."

It was a hard truth, but he could so easily have lied that she appreciated his candor. "Then how could you *want* to make love to me?" she asked.

He looked as confused as she felt. "I guess because love survives in spite of everything." Then he smiled grimly. "I'm full of anger and resentment and all kinds of other negative emotions, but at the heart of it all—at *my* heart—is something you gave me on that mountain that's with me still." He frowned. "Is it critical that we understand it?"

It wasn't. She'd heard all she wanted to hear. "Love survives in spite of everything." He loved her.

She wrapped her arms around him and leaned into him, determined that he would never regret this moment, whether or not it led to a reconciliation.

They undressed each other without hurry, then Darrick frowned over the large, colorful bruises on her arm and her hip. He caught her elbow gently in his hand and rubbed his thumb lightly over the remnant of her fall.

"It's all right," she assured him. "It doesn't hurt anymore."

"It looks painful."

"It isn't."

He raised his frowning glance to her eyes. "You're sure you're all right to do this?"

"Yes. I'm sure."

"Okay." Darrick caught her hand and brought her with him to the side of the new bed where he tossed back the coverlet and the top sheet.

"Maybe we should use the sleeping bag and the air mattress on the floor," she said with a small laugh. "I mean, this *is* your parents' bed."

He swung her up into his arms and placed her in the middle of it. "We can consider it a sort of ritual blessing."

Then he was beside her, they were body to body and she could think of nothing but what it was like to be in his arms again after the interminable time that had separated them—the lost months, the pretended recovery from childbirth, the anger.

His body was like suede against hers, both rough and smooth as he held her to him and explored every curve and plane of her body.

She ran her fingertips over his shoulders, his muscled back, the straight line of his spine to the back of his waist.

Her hands became unsteady as a fire line began to form under her skin in the wake of his touch. He hitched her leg up over his and traced up the line of her thigh, over her hip, then back again.

She raised her mouth to his and kissed him hungrily,

slipping her hand up between them to trace the pattern of hair across his chest, down to his waist, and lower.

He leaned up on an elbow and cradled her in his arm, returning her kisses as he filled his free hand with one of her breasts, exploring its shape until the tip pearled in his hand.

Then his hand moved down the center of her body, over the concavity of her stomach to the warm juncture of her thighs. Her body lifted toward him of its own accord.

Darrick felt her hand close over him, and pleasure rushed at him like a train without a brake, like something with the potential to run him down.

He wanted more time, but he felt as though the air around him was already on fire. He turned onto his back and pulled her over him, careful of the bruise on her hip.

He took her hands to steady her as she settled over him and he entered her.

Pleasure hit him with the impact of that runaway train. It pinned him to the mattress, rode over and over him, then did it again for good measure.

He cried out his surprise, but the sound was lost to him in the high-pitched series of gasps Skye uttered as she tightened around him and the whole world seemed to convulse and fly apart.

Skye's fingers were laced in Darrick's, and she clung to him, prepared to relive every wonderful pleasure of their night in the shelter of the tarpaulin.

But this was different. Fulfillment came upon her with all the intensity of that night, but it took her deeper, flung her higher and lasted longer, and she could only conclude that it was the result of what they'd been through together in the past few weeks.

They'd fed and rocked babies side by side, they'd stared at each other sleepily across the kitchen table, while Michelle and Gabrielle demanded more food, more rocking, more something they couldn't explain.

They'd scrubbed and painted with camaraderie, they'd made friends of the Fishers together, and they'd sat on the porch steps arm in arm and watched the sunset.

This was their bodies' expression of what their hearts and souls already knew. They loved each other. They were good together.

As the world around her began to subside, Skye looked down into Darrick's dark eyes and wondered with a little stab of fear if she'd just imagined all that in a rush of emotion.

But she hadn't. His eyes were filled with love for her as he raised a hand to tuck her hair behind her ear. But he'd admitted before that he loved her. The question was, would he ever be able to forgive her?

She turned her lips into the hand he now held to her cheek. "I'm sorry, Darrick," she whispered. "I'm so sorry."

He pulled her down into his arms and kissed her fiercely. "You're forgiven," he said.

"What?" she whispered.

"I love you," he said.

She was so filled with happiness she wanted to laugh and cry. She wanted to give him things. The sun, the moon, every particle of herself....

Her happy thoughts stopped abruptly as she realized with a jolt that she was forgetting something critical in her perfect family formula.

She could give Darrick everything she had with open-hearted generosity, but she still couldn't give him children. And he was wonderful with them. He should have them. Several of them.

Her joy fell in on itself like a jolted soufflé.

DARRICK WRAPPED his arms around her as all his emotional struggles of the past few days dissolved into nothingness. He totally forgave her, exonerated and reclaimed her.

Intellectually he'd been able to resist the love he still felt for her despite the tricks she'd played because he'd been able to think about how she'd wronged him.

But that long-awaited lovemaking hadn't left room for thought. It had been pure emotion, pure physical statement and response. I love you. You love me. Nothing can stand against that. The train will knock it down.

Every negative thought he'd held was gone. He was free. He felt as though he shimmered.

He held Skye so tightly that he was aware of the instant when the joy he'd seen in her eyes only a moment ago was replaced by something that made her stiffen and grow suddenly cold.

He pulled the sheet over them and eased her into the crook of his arm. Her cheeks were white, her eyes evading his.

He braced himself over her, caught her chin in his hand and held it steady until she was forced to look at him. "What?" he asked. "You can't tell me that wasn't the most incredible half hour of your entire lifetime."

She gave him a sorry attempt at a smile. "No, I can't. It was probably the most incredible half hour of a few other lifetimes as well."

"Then, what?"

"Dori will be home soon," she said, trying to push against him to get up.

He held her down with a hand on her shoulder, fighting a niggling feeling of impending doom. "What? What else haven't you told me?"

She lay back docilely and tried to force another smile, but in her eyes he saw hopelessness. "Nothing," she replied. "I've told you everything and that was—" her eyes filled and her voice grew thick but she finished quietly "—certainly worth waiting nine months to experience again. But..." She sat up abruptly, and he found himself looking at her naked back, the slightly slumped line of her shoulders under her glossy dark hair and the delicate, crenelated line of her spine. "I married you for the twins," she said bravely now that she didn't have to face him, "but soon one of your brothers will be home to claim them."

He didn't believe her for a minute, but he didn't understand what game she was playing, either.

"So you're going to hold out for Dillon or Duncan?" he asked. "Whoever fathered the twins?"

She gave him a reprimanding look over her shoulder, then stood and pulled her shirt on. "Of course not. I'm going home."

"You live with me," he reminded her.

She collected the rest of her clothes. "Not anymore. With all the lies I told you, you have easy grounds for divorce."

"What if I don't want a divorce?"

"You will when you come to your senses." She threw her clothes in the hamper and went to the doorway. "I'm going to shower," she said. "Think about what you want for dinner."

He sat in the middle of the bed, wondering what in the hell had happened. That lovemaking had been magical, she'd sat astride him beaming with love and happiness, fallen into his arms, and suddenly the entire outlook of his future had changed.

Well. He couldn't do anything about the problem until he understood what it was, and she wouldn't tell him if he pushed her. So he decided the wisest course of action was to let her think she'd won, then let his family work her over with their love and good cheer and complete inability to take no for an answer.

Chapter Thirteen

The quiet beach house was pandemonium the moment Darrick's parents arrived pulling a U-haul trailer. They'd also picked up Harper Harriman, who came through the front door carrying two large grocery bags.

"What happened to your aunt?" Skye asked.

Harper smiled. "She's fine. This time my Aunt Cleo from Baltimore is staying with her."

Skye took one of the bags from her, studying the woman's face for any telling similarities to the babies'. Perhaps it was there in her smile? "How nice for your aunt to have *two* sisters."

Harper raised an eyebrow as they headed side by side toward the kitchen. "My aunt has *four* sisters. They had a singing group as girls."

"You're kidding! How exciting."

Darrick closed the door and discovered in a matter of minutes that he'd lost whatever meager control he'd had over his life.

Skye took over the kitchen, Dori and Harper took over the twins, the Fishers saw the car arrive, came over with several cots they'd promised to lend him and stayed to play cards with his parents at the kitchen table.

He needed a dog, he told himself as he carried in luggage. After a brief career as a family man, he'd discovered that he was no longer a father, and if his wife had anything to say about it, he was going to lose his status as husband, also.

His father and Cliff came out to help him unload the trailer.

"Your mother insisted," Charlie explained, "that with this many extra people and no furniture, we were going to need things to sit on."

They pulled out two new woven lawn chairs, a gaudily painted china elephant table that stood about two feet high, an ice-cream parlor chair with a wire back in the shape of a heart and a seat upholstered in a pink-and-white stripe, an oak bench with a carved back that had to be a mistake because it was actually very nice looking, and a Boston rocker with a tie-on chartreuse seat cushion.

Charlie hauled out a brand-new gas grill. "Our gift to the house," he said, handing it to Darrick.

It was a deluxe model with three separate burners under the grill and a small fold-out wooden shelf attached to the side. "This is great, Dad. Thank you."

"Don't thank me, just fix me a juicy burger. I'm on this low-cholesterol, low-taste, low-fun diet."

Darrick studied him in concern. "Doctor's orders?"

Charlie shook his head. "No. Orders straight from the top."

Cliff picked up the ice-cream chair. "*God* put you on a low-fat diet?" he asked in disbelief.

Charlie shook his head. "No, Peg did."

Darrick picked up a pile of woven rope in a clear plastic bag in a corner of the trailer and held it up. "What's this?" he asked his father.

"A Hatteras hammock," Charlie said. "Got it for a bargain from a neighbor. I hope you have a couple of trees in the back."

A hammock. He carried it out to the backyard after he'd helped get everything else inside. If he was right, the ash tree should be just far enough from the apple tree for this to work.

It was! He tied the ends of the hammock in place, opened out the netting, then sat carefully in it and bounced a little to test its stability. Satisfied that it would hold, he raised his legs and eased them into the woven pod.

He understood instantly why the hammock was the symbol of summer leisure. It was like lying suspended on a cloud. He tucked his hands behind his head and closed his eyes. Yes. This could be the life.

"To complete the picture," Skye's voice said, "you should have a book open on your chest and a lemonade in your hand."

He took it as a good sign that she'd come out to him, and the light note in her voice was like a balm over his concerns. "Can you get them for me?" he asked without opening his eyes. "I don't think I can move."

"Not a chance." He felt her walk around the hammock, probably inspecting it. "Your parents are insisting on taking us all out for dinner, but I made two pans of lasagna and don't think they should spend the money. We need your vote."

"It's always safer to let my mother do what she wants to do. They'll be here for three days. We can have the lasagna tomorrow night."

"Your mother says you're going to barbecue tomorrow afternoon."

"Then the night after."

He felt her give the hammock a little rock. "Will you be joining us for dinner, then, or are we supposed to bring you something back?"

He opened one eye to look up at her. The sun was low and she was all ivory skin and dark hair against a sky darkening toward dusk.

"Depends," he said. "Are you going to behave like a loving wife, or are you going to just give me those tragic looks that could make even a passerby cry?"

Curiously, much of the tension was gone between them and they'd developed a weird ability to discuss the collapse of their lives with a friendly detachment.

"What tragic looks?" she asked indignantly.

"Go look in the mirror," he said. "You're wearing one right now. It's the I-can't-take-it-and-I'm-headed-for-the-Klondike look."

She slapped one of his protruding elbows. "Don't bad-mouth Olivia. And Mariposa isn't as dramatic as the Klondike."

"It serves the purpose," he replied. "You had a tragic beginning, and you're determined to make the rest of your life a tragedy, as well. Or why would you have done something as outrageous as pretend to be the mother of the twins?"

"I explained that," she said, fiddling with a knot in the weave of the hammock. "And it's useless to go over it again. Are you coming to dinner or not?"

"Unless you promise not to do the look, I don't see the point."

He thought he had her when she heaved an exasperated sigh. She was going to have to tell him why she was so sure things couldn't work out between them.

But she turned toward the house instead and shouted, "Ladies!"

There was a thunder of feet headed toward him, but before he could find purchase on the rocky hammock to turn and see what was happening, Dori and Harper had reached him, mischief in their eyes.

"What?" he asked, threading his fingers in the hammock in instinctive trepidation.

"He'd rather stay here than join us for dinner," Skye told her companions.

"Hammock potato!" Dori accused.

"Name calling accomplishes nothing," Harper said, taking hold of the end of the hammock on his left side. "This requires action."

"Don't you…" he began to threaten, but before he could finish, his wife had the middle of the hammock and Dori, the other end.

In an instant he was on his stomach on the grass.

"All right, that's it!" He scrambled to his feet and women went screaming in all directions. That, he thought with some genetic memory culled from his Highlander ancestors, was what a man's life should be all about.

Dinner was loud and wild. The McKeons, the Fishers and Harper took up a long table in one corner of a restaurant perched on a rocky headland just south of Dancer's Beach.

The laughter was uproarious as Charlie recounted for Bertie and Cliff the story of his sons' burping contest during the lawn party all those years ago.

Darrick noted that Skye listened greedily, but failed to laugh along with everyone else. And he didn't think anyone else would notice it, but under her interested expression was that look of loss she'd worn since almost the moment after they'd made love.

He'd have given his old age, he thought, to understand what was on her mind.

"How do you put up with being married to a McKeon?" Harper teased Skye from the other end of the table. Darrick sat at the head of the table, and Skye at a right angle to him so that the baby carrier could be placed between them. She patted his arm affectionately. "He's actually a very sweet Neanderthal," she said.

Peg heaved a long-suffering sigh. "It's all Charlie's fault. I tried to teach them good manners, but those fishing trips with their father undermined all my efforts. All they packed was one change of clothes apiece for ten days and cases of sardines and Cheez Whiz. How can civility possibly survive under those conditions?" She patted Dori's arm. "One trip with them did it for Dori. She never wanted to go again."

"I discovered," Dori said, looking around the table at her interested audience. "That my father was actually the architect of the burping competition."

Charlie shrugged, apparently experiencing little guilt. "I did teach them never to do it in public. It isn't my fault that that concession to polite behavior didn't take."

More stories and more laughter were served with dessert, and the evening finally ended with an invitation to the Fishers to join them for the following day's barbecue.

With Darrick's parents sleeping in the downstairs bedroom, he and Skye moved the air mattress and the sleeping bag into the upstairs room. Dori and Harper slept on cots in the front room Dillon had chosen.

Harper picked up her things and was going to move them when she learned the room was earmarked for Dillon, but Dori rolled her eyes at her. "Oh, come on. That's carrying a grudge a little too far. Dillon's never even slept in this room. Put your stuff down."

"What happened between Dillon and Harper, anyway?" Skye asked when she and Darrick had moved the portable crib into their room and closed the door behind them.

"He wouldn't talk about it." He shook the zipped-together sleeping bags over the air mattress. "And neither would she. All I know is that they're furious with each other."

Skye dropped the pillows she carried onto the air mattress. "I really like her."

"We all do," he said. "We used to hope they'd resolve the problem, but it doesn't look promising."

"Too bad."

"Yeah," he said. "That's what happens when people won't talk to each other."

Skye sighed and gave him a look intended to stop that turn in the conversation. "Darrick, it's late. Please don't start."

"*You* started it," he countered, peering into the crib and finding both babies sleeping with cherubic little smiles. "But you seem to think you can just call a halt in the middle."

"Darrick." She caught his arms and stopped him in the middle of the dark room. "We've said all there is to say."

He took her arms and gave her a small shake. "What do you mean?" he demanded, keeping his voice down in deference to the babies and Dori and Harper down the hall. "As I recall, you're the one who got to do all the talking. You spent a long time explaining to me why you tricked me about the twins, and when I could finally come around to understanding all that and felt ready to move on, you told me you were leaving. I think there's a little something wrong with this sequence.''

She pulled him down to sit with her on top of the sleeping bag. ''Darrick, did you miss what I told you when I explained why I wanted the babies so badly?''

''I didn't miss anything. You said you had a ruptured appendix, your husband left you...''

''I'm sterile!'' she said in a loud whisper. He saw the moonlight through the bare window pick out the curve of her cheeks and chin, and the tip of her nose. ''Sterile! I can't have babies!''

He nodded. ''Right. I got that.''

Now she stared at him. ''Are you sure?'' she asked impatiently though quietly. ''If you wanted to have children with me, you'd have to go to a fertility clinic where you could fertilize some other woman's egg and have *her* carry the baby.''

''Doesn't that paint a scene right out of *From Here to Eternity*,'' he said drily. ''That would not be *our* baby.''

''My point precisely. We can not have *our* baby.''

''We can adopt a baby.''

She put her hands to her eyes. ''I thought about that, and I know I could love any baby, but your family...''

Now she was beginning to annoy him. ''My family can love any baby.''

''Listen to me,'' she said urgently. ''Your family is wonderful. I know that. But you're so close and you enjoy so much being together.''

''How would adopting a baby change that?''

"Say we got a little boy who didn't like to fish. It would ruin your family fishing trips for you."

"Skye." Elbows on his knees he leaned toward her. "Duncan hated to fish, but he came along because he loved us. He sat on the bank and read or hiked and explored. Trust me. No one ruins a good time for my family, and I defy anyone who joins them at anything to have a *bad* time."

"You're thinking idealistically."

"I'm telling you what I know from experience."

"You're wrong," she insisted. "I lived without the wonderful connection you have to your family, and I won't let you risk it."

"You've got another flawed theory, Skye." He caught her arm and held her there as she tried to get to her feet and evade his rebuttal. "Since you haven't had a loving family, maybe you shouldn't judge how they work. You don't have to be a clone to be accepted. My family would love a child of ours because we loved him, even if he would rather play with his Nintendo than go fishing. And, anyway, you're sure that's the problem?"

She looked at him blankly. "What do you mean?"

"Well, for someone who lied through her teeth to get into this relationship, you're finding a million excuses to get out. Maybe I just never figured as prominently in the deal as the babies did."

"Don't be ridi—"

"Or maybe after a couple of weeks of being up half the night and never having a moment that's really all yours, you're deciding that motherhood isn't what you want after all."

"I loved…"

"After all those years of living without love," he

interrupted again, "maybe now that you've seen it close up, you're thinking it's just too much trouble, after all. You end up with horse collars on your wall, well-intentioned people barging in and out of your space, someone else you have to explain yourself to when it was all once so simple. When you were alone and life got out of hand, you just got in your plane and left your problems on the ground."

"Are you through?" she asked tightly.

"Yes." It was a desperate measure, but he'd come this far. It was all or nothing. He took his wedding ring off, forced it into the palm of her hand and closed her fingers over it. "I am. I'll explain it all to my family, and you can go home to the clouds. Go to sleep." He snatched up a pillow. "I'll sleep in Duncan's room."

WELL, THIS WAS *what I wanted,* Skye told herself as she tossed and turned and wept all night long. She had wanted to make up to Darrick for the awful deception by saving him for some other woman who could give him all the things she couldn't.

He couldn't see it now, but it was the right thing for him.

And it was the right thing for her. She could go back to Mariposa and pick up where she'd left off.

She realized with a painful sigh that she couldn't do that. Too much had changed. *She* had changed.

She was no longer the lonely waif who'd grown into a lonely woman without knowing what it was like to be loved. She'd been a wife and a mother—only briefly—but those roles had changed the essence of her being.

She was good at the give-and-take that love required. If she'd resumed her relationship with Darrick from a base of honesty, she was sure they'd have made it.

Now she would have to find work that wasn't so solitary. Maybe the freight service would have to become a passenger service. Yes.

She tried to cheer herself with the thought of carrying travelers to regular stops in San Francisco, Sacramento, Los Angeles, San Diego. But her mind kept thinking of destinations north—Edenfield and Dancer's Beach.

She would have turned her face into her pillow and wept but Michelle awoke.

DARRICK WENT downstairs at the crack of dawn, planning to make himself bacon and eggs and to brood over the course of action he'd chosen last night. He'd been sure his accusations would bring Skye around, that she would rethink her conviction that he wouldn't be happy with an adopted child and come running to Duncan's room to tell him.

But the night wore on with agonizing slowness, and he hadn't heard a sound from their room. Except for the babies, who'd each awakened once and apparently gone promptly back to sleep after being fed.

His plans for a solitary breakfast went down in flames when he detected the aroma of coffee brewing and something else cooking he couldn't quite identify. He found his mother at the stove and his father sitting at the table with the newspaper open across it.

The last thing Darrick wanted at that moment was conversation, but he reminded himself that this was the very type of situation he'd chided Skye about last night.

He went to kiss his mother on the cheek and peered over her shoulder at the strange looking strips of something in the frying pan.

"What is that?" he asked.

"Turkey bacon," she said, reaching up to pat him on the cheek. "You'll like it."

"Turkeys don't make bacon," he felt called upon to tell her.

"Well, pigs don't make bacon, either, Darrick, people make it out of pigs. Only these people made it out of turkeys. It's good for you."

From the table his father looked up at him commiseratingly over the rims of his glasses. "Don't fight it. Then she'll be treating you for ulcers as well as high cholesterol."

Darrick watched as she took a small carton out of the refrigerator.

"I don't have high cholesterol," he said. "What's *that?*"

His mother pointed to the table with the carton. "Go sit down. It's egg substitute. You can't tell scrambled eggs made with this from the real thing."

"But I like my eggs fried. Over easy."

"You'll get them scrambled."

His father beckoned him toward the table and handed him the Sports section.

His mother finally came to the table with a plate in each hand and balancing a third on her arm like a waitress in a busy truck stop.

She went back to the counter for the coffeepot, then sat beside Charlie opposite Darrick.

"What's wrong between you and Skye?" she asked while he was still analyzing the edibility of the stuff on his plate.

He picked up his fork, in no mood for questions. "Nothing," he said, stabbing the mound of scrambled whatever to check its consistency.

"She came downstairs during the night, made a cup of tea and had a good cry," his mother reported. "It didn't sound like 'nothing.'"

He looked up in surprised dismay. "I didn't hear her."

His mother raised an eyebrow while his father shook the newspaper he held and raised it a little higher. "You're in a sleeping bag. How could she have gotten out of it without waking you up?"

He leaned over his plate toward her. "With all love and respect, Mom, none of your business."

"You're my business," she said, seemingly unoffended by the rebuff. "She's yours, and therefore also my business."

He resigned himself suddenly to the inevitable fact that he had to tell them sometime, so it might as well be now. "Well, that's where you're wrong. She doesn't consider herself mine." He ate a bite of egg because he was now too preoccupied to taste it, anyway. She'd cried? Was that good or bad?

"She looks at you like you're a gift from heaven. What are you talking about?"

He put his fork down, took a sip of coffee and explained that she hadn't given birth to the twins.

His mother studied him steadily, then leaned back in her chair and also seemed to need her coffee. His father lowered the paper and took off his glasses.

"How did you find out?" his father asked.

Darrick explained about the fall from the attic ladder.

"But…why did she lie?"

He told them about the name D. K. McKeon on the birth certificate and how the staff had presumed the babies were his.

"She's unable to have children. By the way she reacted when I showed up with them at the airport, I thought for sure they were hers…ours. Anyway, when I accused her of having abandoned them, she saw it as her opportunity to *have* babies. So she took it."

Darrick watched his mother's eyes fill with tears and covered her hand with his. "It's all right. You haven't lost them. They just belong to Dillon or Duncan, not to me."

She turned her hand in his to squeeze it. "I was worried about you, not about us. I'm sorry. I know how much you love the babies."

He had to draw a breath before he could speak, the pain in his gut finally minimized by the knowledge that the twins would still be in the family.

"It's all right," he said. "I'll be their uncle."

"Are you unable to forgive Skye?"

"I can. I have. But she's convinced that I won't be happy with an adopted baby."

"Why on earth not?"

He related her theory about the child who wouldn't like to fish and how that would impact upon their family outings.

"That's ridiculous," his father said. "Duncan hated to fish, but he always—"

Darrick cut him off with a nod. "I told her that, but she's determined. And I'm wondering if maybe she isn't just wanting out. I can't believe she'd be this adamant about it if she wanted to find a way to stay with me."

"Unless it's some kind of compensation," his father suggested, "for tricking you in the first place."

"And if she loves you," his mother added, "and my every instinct tells me that she does, she wants what's best for you. And in her mind, that's a woman with whom you can have children."

"But I want *her.*"

His father nodded, his expression empathetic. "A loving woman gives you what she thinks you need whether you want it or not—a fertile woman, turkey bacon, same principle. All in the name of devotion. Ow!"

His father's philosophy had earned him a sock in the arm.

Chapter Fourteen

"You're sure there's nothing we can do?" Dori watched Skye peel potatoes. "I'm not a great cook, but I can peel and chop."

Skye smiled at her, feeling as though she'd finally pulled herself together. She'd done the right thing about Darrick. It hurt like hell now, but years down the road when he sent her a Christmas card with his family portrait that included a beautiful wife, and two girls and a boy all dressed in matching outfits, it would...well, it would still hurt like hell, but she'd know she'd done what was best for him.

"No, everything's under control. This potato salad won't take long at all. But it'll be another hour and a half before we eat. Why don't you and Harper take a walk to town, or along the beach?"

"Can we take the twins?" Harper asked. She stood on Skye's other side, making smiling faces into the baby carrier on the counter. Both twins smiled gummily. "It's nice and warm and you'd both love that, wouldn't you?"

"Sure." Skye leaned into the babies' view and smiled, too. Their little smiles widened even more in response to her, and she wondered if she would be able to hold her emotions in check until this weekend was over and she could go back to Mariposa. "They've just been fed and changed so they should be happy."

In a few moments Dori and Harper headed off to town, pushing the baby carriage. Skye relaxed for the first time that morning. Her smiling face required considerable willpower to maintain.

Charlie and Peg had gone to the Fishers' to inspect a dry sink they were anxious to sell, and Darrick was outside setting up the grill. She was alone in the house.

She poured herself a glass of wine and sipped it as she cut up the potatoes and put them on to boil.

Darrick jolted her out of her sense of control by opening the screen door in the back and peering in at her.

"Got to run to the store for steak sauce. You need anything?"

"No, thanks," she said, turning back to her task. Looking at him was just too hard.

"Want to kiss me goodbye?"

"No, thanks," she said again, still turned resolutely away.

"Then, will you form the burgers for me, please?"

The door closed and she felt all her meticulously built reserve collapse into despair.

She went to the refrigerator for the burger meat mixed with onions and pepper and all sort of other tasty additions Charlie had added to it and placed it on the counter. Then she took down a platter, placed waxed paper on it, and removed her ring and put it on the side of the sink.

She patted the fragrant mixture between her hands and thought about how much she would miss Darrick's family. They were everything hers had been too self-involved to be, and it felt a little like being offered water when you were dying of thirst and having it taken away after just one drop on your tongue.

But she knew what was best for Darrick.

She turned her mind to thoughts of redecorating her apartment in Mariposa. That would help. She would paint it white and buy wicker furniture and haunt secondhand stores and antique shops for monstrous old things no one else wanted…

It took a moment for her to realize the game her brain was playing. It was putting her back in Dancer's Beach.

All right. She would think about Olivia. In the evenings, with free time on her hands, she could research dancers in the Klondike and see if she could find out what happened to Olivia and whether or not Barton ever found her.

She even wondered if Darrick would let her take the bodice home with her. He had no use for it, wasn't captivated by it as she was.

She decided that wouldn't be fair. If Olivia had left it—she'd left it *here*. Skye had simply been mistaken in what Olivia had intended it to accomplish. It hadn't been meant to save her marriage to Darrick.

Perhaps it had been meant for one of his brothers. Then it occurred to her in a flash of insight. Harper! It was intended for Dillon and Harper, who might be the twins' parents.

She was completely into the idea of the bodice somehow bringing those two warring parties back together when she reached toward the faucet to wash her hands and noticed that the spot where her ring had been was an empty expanse of white porcelain.

She stared at it for a moment, as though that would make it reappear. And when it didn't, she noticed that the bowl from which she'd been scooping out handfuls of hamburger mix had been nudged toward the back of the counter. That the plastic bottle of dish detergent that stood behind it had fallen onto its side and most probably knocked her ring off into the sink.

But there was nothing in the sink—except the dark hole of the old open drain.

"No!" she whispered to herself as the emotional control she'd built and rebuilt several times today exploded like Vesuvius.

DARRICK PULLED into the driveway with his small grocery bag of A-1 Sauce and Raisinettes.

He intended to bypass the kitchen and go straight to the backyard since there was little point in telling Skye he was back. She didn't seem to care what he did—or was working very hard to create that impression.

But he heard the sound of deep, wrenching sobs through the screen.

He set the bag down on the grill table and ran up the steps.

"Skye?" he called yanking the door open. "What happened?"

Water puddled around Skye, who lay on her stomach near the sink.

His heart leaped into his throat as he went toward her. He tried to imagine what had happened. Had she been attacked? Fallen? Sustained a shock of some kind?

As he got closer he saw that she was halfway under the sink. What had made very little sense when he'd walked in the back door made even less sense now.

But he wasn't concerned about logic. He was concerned about Skye. He pushed the cupboard doors out of his way and turned her over.

"Skye, are you all right?" he demanded, placing a hand under her waist so that he could ease her out from under the pipes. "What happened?"

She was wet and sobbing hysterically. In her right hand was a wrench from the tool set he kept in the car. In her left was the sink trap.

He took them from her and pulled her to a sitting position. "Are you all right?" he asked again.

"My ring fell down the drain!" she cried, trying to pull away from him to go back to it. "I took it off to make the hamburgers and then it was gone!"

God. Rings. He'd thought she was unconscious or worse, and she'd only lost her ring.

"Easy," he said, trying to calm her. "I'll find it for you. Go change, your shirt is drenched."

"I don't want to change," she said adamantly, "I want to find my ring!"

"I said I'd find it, but I want you to calm down."

"How can I calm down?" she screamed at him, tears streaming down her cheeks. "My ring is down the drain!"

He gave her a small shake, wondering at her near hysteria. "Skye, it's only a ring. If we can't find it I'll buy you a new one."

It wasn't until after he heard the words himself that

he realized the absurdity of them, considering the state of their marriage. Then suddenly *her* emotional state, as the one who was insisting their marriage was over, seemed even more absurd.

But she didn't seem to notice that—at least not in the same way he did.

She was crying noisily, her mouth contorted. "It's not *just* a ring," she wept, "it's a *token!*"

He was about to ask, "A token of what?" when he recalled a snatch of the conversation they'd had the day they'd gone shopping for the ring and she'd said the diamond was too big.

He'd told her he wanted it because it was a token of his feelings for her.

And then he realized what her emotional unraveling at the loss of it meant. Precisely what his father had guessed. She loved him and she was doing what she thought was best for him.

"You have to find it!" she said desperately.

The deliberately loud sound of throat clearing came from behind them. He turned to see his parents and the Fishers standing just inside the back door. The Fishers were staring. His parents were their customary shock-proof selves.

"Cliff and I will find it," his father said with a wink. "You go dry her off."

"Go on upstairs where you can have some…where it's quiet," his mother said. "I'll bring you up some tea in a bit."

Darrick pulled Skye to her feet.

She resisted. "But, I want…"

He considered the merits of brute force compared to reasonable argument and decided on the former.

Reasonable argument had gotten him nowhere so far. He lifted her into his arms and carried her up the stairs and into the bathroom.

He set her on her feet in the middle of the floor and reached under the sink for a thick bath towel.

She pulled her wet clothes off as he soaped a washcloth. She'd stopped crying, but she remained shaken. He saw a piece of ribbon with which she sometimes tied her hair back, knotted around her neck. Hanging from it was *his* wedding ring.

"I was thinking that maybe Olivia left the bodice for Dillon and Harper," she said, dropping her shirt to the floor and reaching behind her to unhook her bra, "instead of for us. And then I noticed it was gone. I found tools in the car and then I got the trap off..."

He withheld a smile. She looked up at him suspiciously. "Don't laugh," she warned, a sudden glimpse of her old self showing through the sniffs and tears.

"I wouldn't think of it," he said gravely. "Come on, get the shorts off so I can wrap you up."

He held the towel open, surprised when she did as he asked. He wrapped her in it, tucking it in under her arm and handing her the washcloth.

When her face was clean, he wrapped another towel around her shoulders and lifted her up to sit her on the counter. She was more composed now but she looked uncertain, as though some new truth had been revealed to her.

He leaned a hand on the counter on either side of her and looked into her eyes.

"You were pretty upset about the ring," he said conversationally.

She stared at him a moment. He guessed she was

analyzing what he meant before she agreed or disagreed.

"Of course I was," she finally ventured carefully. "It was expensive."

"So you were crying because you wanted to give it back to me when you left?"

That measuring look again. "No."

"You wanted to sell it when you got back to Mariposa?"

She evaded his eyes. He moved his head to follow hers.

"No," she said finally.

"Then you were suffering this major trauma…why?"

A pleat formed between her eyebrows. "Because it's my wedding ring."

"But you don't want to be married."

She sighed and a fresh tear fell. He caught a glimpse of that misery he saw so often in her. "Yes, I do."

"But not to me?"

"Yes, to you," she said impatiently, "but I know what's best for you, and that's to be married to someone else."

"You once told me you feel justified in making decisions for me because you love me."

"Yes." She said it confidently, as though it was the backbone of her case. "I love you and I know what's best for you.

He loved it, because that made it the backbone of his.

"Well, if we employ that rule, I can decide what's right for you because *I* love *you*. Right?"

She opened her mouth to reply, then apparently decided that wasn't wise.

"And I think what's right for you is me."

She wanted to concede; he saw it in her eyes. But she'd convinced herself she couldn't win. "Then we're at an impasse," she said.

"Wrong, my love." He cupped her face in his hands and kissed her soundly. "I'm bigger, so my love outweighs yours."

He knew that was wrong, of course. Her love had been big enough to allow her to deny herself what she wanted so that he would have what she thought he wanted.

"Nothing can be bigger than what I feel," she said in a whisper.

"Then how can you consider ignoring it?" He looked into her eyes, knowing that everything he felt for her showed in his.

Skye read love in his gaze and could only stare at it. After all she'd done, he loved her. With the knowledge that she couldn't give him babies, he still loved her. The past receded and a bright future planted itself squarely in her path.

For the first time in her life, she felt truly grounded—not restricted to the ground, but finally connected to it. She had Darrick.

"I can't." She wrapped her arms around him and held him close, tears filling her eyes again. "But are you *sure?*"

"Unshakably sure." He hugged the breath out of her. "Now can I have my ring back?"

"Oh." Skye pulled the knot in the ribbon toward the front, and Darrick untied it, letting the ring slip off into Skye's palm. She put it back on his finger. "I promise to love you *un*selfishly this time."

He pulled her into his arms again. "Wanting babies is hardly a selfish motive for love."

She drew back to look into his face. "I wanted them," she admitted. "But I wanted you every bit as much."

He smiled gently. "I know. And now you've got me."

A tear spilled over, and she wrapped her arms around him, leaning into him. "I'm sorry the twins aren't ours. But we have them until your brothers come home, then we'll adopt our own. Right?"

"Right. We haven't lost anything. We just got to share in a very special gift."

"And we'll continue to share in it when their father comes home—whoever he is."

"We found it!" The shout came loudly and clearly from downstairs. "Skye! We found it!"

Skye sagged against Darrick in relief. "Oh, thank God!" He lifted her off the counter and waited while she pulled on jeans and a T-shirt. Then they hurried downstairs to where Peg sloshed the ring in bottled water while Charlie reconnected the sink trap with moral support from Cliff. Someone had mopped up the floor.

Dori and Harper had returned with the twins and were watching the action.

Peg wiped off the ring with a paper towel, then held it out to Skye.

Darrick intercepted it and slipped it back on her finger. "Only it should be a carat bigger," he said.

"Because my love's even bigger than it was when we bought this."

As he kissed her again, Harper turned to Dori. "Now, why couldn't I have met *him* before I met Dillon?"

"Because fate," Peg replied, "decided you were perfect for Dillon."

Harper bounced Michelle in her arms. "Fate had nothing to do with it. He crashed into me."

"Crashes can be manifestations of fate." Skye took the fussy baby from her. "Fuel pumps on a plane almost never malfunction, yet mine did. And if it hadn't, I'd have dropped Darrick at the airport in San Diego and probably never seen him again. Instead...we were forced to spend time together, to get to know each other."

Harper studied them, sympathy in her eyes. "Peg was explaining about the twins and...everything. I'm sorry."

Darrick took the still-fussing baby from Skye. "Don't be," he said. "These babies have the most devoted family on the planet. We just don't know who their parents are. And Skye and I are going to be fine."

"I'm glad to hear that."

Dori rocked Gabrielle, who still slept, and smiled warmly at Skye. "So am I."

There was a sudden clatter from across the house at the front door, and a male voice shouted, "Hi! Hey, I picked up a picnic table at Costmart! Can somebody help me? Darrick? Dad?"

The voice grew louder as footsteps sounded across the living room, the dining room, approaching the kitchen.

Peg and Dori squealed delightedly, turned in the direction of the voice. Charlie pushed out from under the sink. Harper went pale.

A tall, vibrant man in jeans and a gray sweatshirt with the message Contents under Pressure stopped in the doorway. He had shaggy dark hair, cocoa brown eyes, and a smile Skye immediately identified as belonging to a McKeon.

She might have wondered which brother he was if his smile hadn't died the instant he set eyes on Harper.

This was Dillon.

Take 2 bestselling love stories FREE

Plus get a FREE surprise gift!

Special Limited-Time Offer

Mail to Harlequin Reader Service®

3010 Walden Avenue
P.O. Box 1867
Buffalo, N.Y. 14240-1867

YES! Please send me 2 free Harlequin American Romance® novels and my free surprise gift. Then send me 4 brand-new novels every month, which I will receive months before they appear in bookstores. Bill me at the low price of $3.34 each plus 25¢ delivery and applicable sales tax, if any.* That's the complete price, and a saving of over 10% off the cover prices—quite a bargain! I understand that accepting the books and gift places me under no obligation ever to buy any books. I can always return a shipment and cancel at any time. Even if I never buy another book from Harlequin, the 2 free books and the surprise gift are mine to keep forever.

154 HEN CH7E

Name _____ (PLEASE PRINT)

Address _____ Apt. No. _____

City _____ State _____ Zip _____

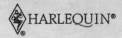 HARLEQUIN®

Not The Same Old Story!

 HARLEQUIN PRESENTS®

Exciting, glamorous
romance stories that take
readers around the world.

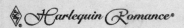 *Harlequin Romance*®

Sparkling, fresh and ten-
der love stories that
bring you pure romance.

 HARLEQUIN® *Temptation*

Bold and adventurous—
Temptation is strong women,
bad boys, great sex!

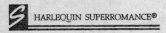 HARLEQUIN SUPERROMANCE®

Provocative and realistic
stories that celebrate life
and love.

 HARLEQUIN AMERICAN ROMANCE®

Contemporary
fairy tales—where
anything is possible
and where dreams
come true.

 HARLEQUIN® INTRIGUE®

Heart-stopping, suspenseful
adventures that combine the
best of romance and mystery.

 LOVE & LAUGHTER™

Humorous and romantic stories
that capture the lighter side of
love.

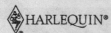 

HARLEQUIN ULTIMATE GUIDES™

A series of how-to books for today's woman.

Act now to order some of these extremely
helpful guides just for you!

*Whatever the situation, Harlequin Ultimate Guides™
has all the answers!*

#80507	HOW TO TALK TO A	$4.99 U.S. ☐	
	NAKED MAN	$5.50 CAN.☐	
#80508	I CAN FIX THAT	$5.99 U.S. ☐	
		$6.99 CAN.☐	
#80510	WHAT YOUR TRAVEL AGENT	$5.99 U.S. ☐	
	KNOWS THAT YOU DON'T	$6.99 CAN.☐	
#80511	RISING TO THE OCCASION		
	More Than Manners: Real Life	$5.99 U.S. ☐	
	Etiquette for Today's Woman	$6.99 CAN.☐	
#80513	WHAT GREAT CHEFS	$5.99 U.S. ☐	
	KNOW THAT YOU DON'T	$6.99 CAN.☐	
#80514	WHAT SAVVY INVESTORS	$5.99 U.S. ☐	
	KNOW THAT YOU DON'T	$6.99 CAN.☐	
#80509	GET WHAT YOU WANT OUT OF	$5.99 U.S. ☐	
	LIFE—AND KEEP IT!	$6.99 CAN.☐	

(quantities may be limited on some titles)

TOTAL AMOUNT $
POSTAGE & HANDLING $
($1.00 for one book, 50¢ for each additional)
APPLICABLE TAXES* $ _____
TOTAL PAYABLE $ _____
(check or money order—please do not send cash)

To order, complete this form and send it, along with a check or money
order for the total above, payable to Harlequin Ultimate Guides, to:
In the U.S.: 3010 Walden Avenue, P.O. Box 9047, Buffalo, NY
14269-9047; **In Canada:** P.O. Box 613, Fort Erie, Ontario, L2A 5X3.

Name: _____

Address: _____ City: _____

State/Prov.: _____ Zip/Postal Code: _____

*New York residents remit applicable sales taxes.
Canadian residents remit applicable GST and provincial taxes.

◆ HARLEQUIN®

Look us up on-line at: http://www.romance.net   HNFBL4

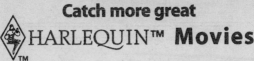